His mind had this silly, worrying tendency to wander away from anything to do with work

What is the matter with you? he asked himself furiously, finding himself doodling a face on his blotter. Big eyes, warm mouth...James scribbled blackly all over it and put down his pen. He would not, must not think about Patience Kirby.

Dear Reader,

Traditionally, a romance novel is seen through a
woman's eyes, but I have often wondered how her
man sees the same events. Are men more like us
than we realize? Are they as unsure of themselves,
are their feelings as deep, do they get hurt, do we
baffle them, keep them awake the way they do us?
Do they need love to make their lives complete?
When Harlequin Presents suggested I write a story
entirely from the man's point of view I jumped at the
chance to find the answers to some of these
questions. I hope you enjoy reading it as much as I
enjoyed writing it.

Sincerely,

Charlotte Lamb

CHARLOTTE LAMB

An Excellent Wife?

MAN Talk

Harlequin Books

TORONTO • NEW YORK • LONDON
AMSTERDAM • PARIS • SYDNEY • HAMBURG
STOCKHOLM • ATHENS • TOKYO • MILAN
MADRID • WARSAW • BUDAPEST • AUCKLAND

ISBN 0-373-11949-6

AN EXCELLENT WIFE?

First North American Publication 1998.

Copyright © 1998 by Charlotte Lamb.

CHAPTER ONE

WHEN the phone began to ring in the outer office James ignored it, expecting his secretary to pick it up, or, failing that, her current assistant, a girl with hair of an improbable yellow, the colour of a day-old chick, which was very suitable since, in his opinion, she had the brains of one, too, not to mention an irritating habit of flinching every time James spoke to her. This morning, however, neither woman answered the phone. The ringing went on and on, without cessation, making it impossible to concentrate on the complex financial analysis he was studying.

At last James could stand the noise no longer. Springing to his feet, he strode to the door of his secretary's office and flung it open. 'Why don't you answer that phone?'

He stopped in mid-sentence, seeing that the room was empty and that there was nobody in the smaller room beyond, the door of which already stood open.

His entire secretarial staff appeared to have deserted him. The place was a *Marie Celeste*. Computers were switched on, their screens blinking, a fax machine was churning out paper in a corner and a pile of letters stood waiting to be signed, but of human beings there was no sign, except for himself, and the still shrill and ringing telephone.

'Where the hell are they?' James leaned across the desk to pick up the phone to silence it, his jet-black hair falling over his eyes. It was getting too long; he must have it trimmed. But he hadn't had time; he was far too busy this week.

'Hallo?' he curtly said, and was met with silence for a second, as if the caller had been taken aback by his impatient tone.

Then a husky female voice said, 'I want to speak to Mr James Ormond, please.'

Miss Roper had a telephone routine which James had heard a thousand times. He followed it now, more or less, not precisely in her words, let alone her cool, clear, modulated tones, in fact more in a terse growl, asking, 'Who is this?'

'My name is Patience Kirby,' she said, as if expecting to be recognised, then added, 'Mr Ormond won't know me, though.'

He'd already realised that. The name meant nothing to him, and if she represented some company she would surely have said so. As she clearly did not, he was not wasting his precious time on her. That was what he employed Miss Roper to do—weed out time-wasting callers and make sure he wasn't inconvenienced. Miss Roper could deal with this woman when she got back.

'Ring back later,' he curtly advised, starting to put the phone down.

Before he could do so, the soft voice implored, 'Oh, please! Is that...? Are *you* Mr Ormond?'

'Ring back later,' he repeated, his cold grey eyes swivelling to stare accusingly at his secretary as she came hurrying through the door with her blonde assistant trailing after her.

Hanging up the phone, James snapped at the two women, 'Why am I having to waste my time answering your phone? Where have you been?'

The blonde girl gave a terrified little baa, like a lamb

confronted by a wolf, and backed out of Miss Roper's office into her own with that halfwitted expression on her face which he recognised all too well. Why on earth had Miss Roper appointed her?

James had gradually got into the habit of leaving the hiring and firing of the secretarial staff to Miss Roper. He had come to trust her judgement, but this girl was not one of her successful appointments. He must have a word on the subject when he wasn't so busy. The girl must go; it was disconcerting to have her backing away from him in such obvious panic every time she saw him. It was making James feel like some relation of Jack the Ripper.

Miss Roper said, 'I'm very sorry, Mr Ormond, the girls in Admin were giving a coffee party for Theresa; we just shot along there with our presents for a few minutes. She's leaving today, as you know...'

'I didn't know. I don't even know her, come to that. Theresa who?'

'Theresa Worth. She's on the switchboard, a girl with short black hair and glasses.'

Dimly James remembered her from that description. 'Oh, that girl! Why is she leaving? Got a better job? Or did you fire her?'

'She's having a baby.'

He raised his brows. 'Is she married?'

His secretary observed him with a wry expression. 'Don't you remember? She got married last year and we gave a party for her. You let us use the canteen.'

'I remember that,' James said, voice cold. They had created havoc in the place, throwing food about, from the sight of the floor, and chucking those paper streamers that fire out of cardboard cases and stick to everything for miles around. The cleaners had complained bitterly next day.

Miss Roper looked guilty, as well she might.

'Is this girl going for good? She isn't just having maternity leave?' asked James.

'No, sir, she and her husband are moving back to Yorkshire. Theresa isn't coming back.'

'Just as well; she seems to have been quite a nuisance so far.'

'She's very popular,' Miss Roper told him indignantly. 'We all like her.' Even if you don't, said her brown eyes. 'And I assure you, Mr Ormond, we weren't gone more than a minute, and I told the switchboard not to put any calls through until we got back. I'm very sorry you were disturbed. I'll investigate and make sure whoever put the call through comes along to apologise in person.'

'No, don't bother, I've already wasted enough time. Just make sure it doesn't happen again.'

'It won't,' she promised, very flushed.

He couldn't remember ever seeing her look so flustered before. She was always so neat and calm, a small sparrow of a woman with brown hair and eyes, who wore a lot of brown, too: brownish tweed skirts in winter, brown linen in summer, with crisp white shirts.

She wore grey and black, too, actually, but whenever James thought about his secretary he imagined her in brown. The colour expressed something essential in her personality. Brenda Roper was older than him by twelve years. When James had begun working at the bank, fourteen years ago, after leaving university, Miss Roper had been assigned to him by his father, then managing director, who had handpicked her from the various candidates, and she had been with James ever since.

In the beginning, when he'd been unsure about himself and struggling to find his feet in a family firm run by a dictatorial father, James had found her efficiency slightly intimidating, which was why he had insisted on calling her Miss Roper, instead of using her first name. Using surnames to each other had seemed to put their relationship on the right footing, made James feel more in charge, less of a newcomer.

They still continued the same polite formality today, although James knew that most of his executives were on first-name terms with their secretaries. From time to time James had hovered on the point of using Brenda Roper's first name, but had always drawn back from changing a long-established and successful habit.

'Why didn't you tell me you were leaving the office?' he demanded. 'Anyone could have walked in here, could have stolen the cash from the safe or operated the computers, retrieved secret information from the private files, endangered one of our projects.'

'Not without the code words, Mr Ormond,' Miss Roper said quietly. 'Nobody can hack into our private computers without those, and you and I are the only ones who know the codes. I'm sorry I didn't tell you we were going out; I didn't want to interrupt you.'

'In that case, why did you both go? You should have left the halfwit behind. At least she can answer phones, even if she can never take a message properly.'

From the outer office they both heard a muffled squeak.

Miss Roper gave James a reproachful look. 'Lisa does her best, Mr Ormond.'

'It isn't good enough!'

'That isn't fair. Believe me, she's a capable girl, she works hard. It's just that you make her nervous.'

'I can't imagine why!'

Miss Roper drew an audible breath, her eyes rounding into brown saucers. She opened her mouth as if to say something, and then the phone began to ring again so she moved swiftly to answer it, looking faintly relieved, like someone snatched from the brink of making a disastrous move.

James walked back into his own office, slamming the door behind him. He had a feeling they had both been rescued from a dangerous moment, too. Sitting down behind his wide, green-leather-topped desk again, he picked up the report he needed to finish studying before lunch. He had the ability to switch off his immediate surroundings and focus all his energy on his work without being distracted by thought of anything else, yet he was always very punctual for appointments. He would stop work at exactly the right moment in order that he should not be late for his lunch with Sir Charles Standish, one of his directors, with whom he needed to discuss the report he was reading.

Charles had once worked for the firm they were studying; he would be able to supply details this report did not contain. James liked to know everything about a company before he made up his mind about it. This particular company might be ripe for a take-over bid by one of the bank's biggest clients, who had asked James for his opinion before they reached a decision. He could not afford to make a mistake.

Miss Roper came in with his coffee five minutes later and began to murmur another apology as she poured strong black coffee from the silver coffee pot on the silver tray, both of them inherited from his father who had always used them.

'I really am very sorry you were disturbed,' she said quietly. 'I know you have a lot on your mind this week.'

Without looking up, James waved a dismissive hand. 'Just make sure it doesn't happen again. In future, there must always be someone on duty out there. I don't pay you to have to answer the phones myself. You'll be wanting me to type my own letters soon!'

'You can't type, Mr Ormond.'

James looked up then, eyes narrowed and wintry, flecked with ice. 'Is that meant to be a joke, Miss Roper? Or was it sarcasm?'

'No, it was simply a statement of fact,' she said, without sounding contrite, and lingered by his desk, as if having more to say.

Impatiently James asked, 'Well?'

'A Miss Kirby is on the phone, sir, asking to speak to you.'

He frowned. 'Kirby?' The name was familiar but he couldn't place it until he remembered the earlier call. 'Patience Kirby?'

Miss Roper gazed at him with eyes that seemed to James to hold a secret, almost furtive smile. 'Yes, that's right, sir, Patience Kirby. Shall I put her through?'

He glared. 'Do you know her?'

'Me?' She looked taken aback. 'No, Mr Ormond, I don't know her. I thought you did.' The secret smile had disappeared from her eyes.

'Well, I don't. Who is she?'

'I've no idea. I didn't ask; I assumed it was a personal call.'

'What gave you that idea?'

'Miss Kirby did.'

'Oh, did she? You don't surprise me. While you were

out I took a call from her, and that was the first time I heard her name.'

'So, shall I put the call through?'

'Certainly not. Find out what she wants and deal with it yourself.'

'Yes, sir.' Miss Roper backed out, closing the door.

James picked up his cup of coffee and sipped as he continued working. It was exactly the way he liked it, strong and fragrant. He always had his coffee at this hour, served in a delicate porcelain cup, white with a dark blue trim edged with gold, one of an early Victorian set which had belonged to his father before him. It was still complete, not a cup or saucer broken, and lived in a glass cabinet when not in use. Bank employees handled it with kid gloves. They knew how much it meant to James Ormond: one of the symbols of continuity in the bank, a link with his dead father and grandfather.

He always drank two cups, ate one thin shortbread biscuit from a flat silver box. He was a man of routine, established very early in life by his father, who had been a strict disciplinarian and who had trained his only son to run the merchant bank, Ormond & Sons, on precisely the lines Henry Ormond's father had laid down some seventy years ago. They might now use new technology, electronic wizardry that made their work much easier, but in other ways nothing much had changed.

Their offices were in the City of London, within walking distance of the rambling outer walls of the Tower of London. From this floor James had a good view of the River Thames and a fascinating panorama of London, old and new. The glint of golden flames on top of the Monument to the Great Fire of London which had destroyed so much of the old city in the reign of Charles the Second, the dome of St Paul's blocking in the skyline behind them, and in front of that the delicate spires of eighteenth-century churches crowded ever closer between the towering glass and concrete of late twentieth-century skyscrapers on both sides of the river.

James Ormond rarely looked at that view and barely saw it if he did occasionally glance out. He rarely looked up from his desk unless he was talking to someone, or was going out of the office. He was always at his desk by the time his secretary arrived; he customarily got to the office by eight and would have liked his secretary to get there by that hour, too, but Miss Roper had a mother living with her for whom she had to get breakfast and who she had to see settled in a chair by the window of their flat, with the television switched on, before she would leave. She paid a neighbour with children at school to come in five days a week to take care of her mother and their flat until she got home.

James had suggested that Miss Roper should get the neighbour to come an hour earlier, but apparently the woman had to get her children off to school first, and the children needed to have a good breakfast and be taken to the school gates in person by their mother. The way these women organised their lives was maddening. It would have been far more convenient if he could have persuaded Miss Roper, and her neighbour, to see things his way, and organise their lives to suit him, but when you came up against their domestic responsibilities these helpful, sensible, capable women became immovable objects, politely deaf to the most rational of arguments.

The phone on his desk rang and James absently reached out a hand to pick it up. 'Yes?'

'Miss Wallis, sir,' his secretary said in the remote voice she always used when she talked about Fiona. James was quite aware that Miss Roper did not like

Fiona, and the hostility was mutual, he suspected, although Fiona was simply cool whenever she mentioned his secretary. Fiona never wasted energy on anyone who was no threat to her. Miss Roper seemed to hum like a vacuum cleaner with unspoken dislike, however.

This morning Fiona sounded listless and fuzzy. 'Darling, I'm sorry, I'll have to cancel dinner tonight. I've got one of my migraines.'

'Cheese or chocolate?'

She laughed huskily. 'You know me too well! Cheese, darling, at dinner last night, with my father. I had the merest sliver of Brie. It looked so delicious I couldn't resist it, and I did hope I'd get away with it this time, but no such luck, alas. I'm almost blind with migraine this morning.'

'How can you be so silly? Why risk triggering a migraine just for a piece of cheese?' It was unlike her to be weak-minded, but she landed herself with one of these migraines every week or two by giving in to a passion for both cheese and chocolate, knowing perfectly well that a migraine would probably follow within eight hours.

'I know, it was crazy, but I had the teeniest bit, James, and I do love Brie.'

His mouth twisted. 'I despair of you. I hope you've at least taken your pills?'

'Just now, but they haven't started working yet. I'm at the office, but I'm going home to lie down in a dark room. It will probably take eight hours for me to get over it, so I have to scrub round this evening. Sorry, James. Maybe tomorrow night?'

'It will have to be Saturday; I'm having dinner with the Jamiesons tomorrow night. Ring me on Saturday morning and don't eat any more cheese! Or chocolate!'

She blew him a kiss. 'I'll be sensible. Bye, darling.'

He hung up, irritated that his planned evening should be ruined by something so unnecessary. They had been going to have dinner at a new restaurant someone had recommended, then go on to a club to dance for an hour or two. It was a favourite way of unwinding for both of them. They both loved the smoky, dark atmosphere of their favourite nightclub.

Fiona, an ice-blonde with hair the texture of white spun sugar and eyes of arctic blue, and he had been seeing each other for a year now, and he knew her family and friends expected them to get engaged any day.

She was probably the most suitable girl James had ever dated, and she would make an excellent wife for a man in his position, but he hadn't proposed yet.

Fiona worked in her father's stockbroking business, had a clear, hard mind for business, was tall and elegant, with perfect taste. He admired her looks, her clothes, her exquisitely furnished flat in Mayfair and her red Aston Martin, about which she was almost passionate—far more excited than she had ever seemed about James, he sometimes thought.

But then he wasn't sure how he felt about her, either. Was he in love with her? He swung his chair round to face the window and gazed at the grey, glittering waters of the Thames, as if they might give him the answer to that question, but honesty forced him to admit to himself that the possibility had never arisen. He had never been 'in love' in his life.

He had fancied girls from time to time, had been to bed with some of them, although not with Fiona, who had told him early on in their relationship that she did not believe in sex before marriage. He had been faintly startled by that, had wondered if she might not be rather cold, sexually, a thought which was faintly offputting. He had tried a few times to get her to change her mind, but when she'd gently refused James hadn't particularly cared. He wasn't desperate to get her into bed, he discovered.

He knew that that meant he wasn't in love with her—but then what did being in love really have to do with getting married? You didn't need to be in love to have a good marriage; all you had to do was choose the right woman.

Someone who shared your interests and attitudes, a beautiful woman like Fiona, who made other men envy you, who looked good at your dinner table, who could discuss international finance or world affairs or politics rationally, without getting emotional or losing her cool. Fiona would never make heavy demands on his time or expect him to change the way his life was organised. What else did he want from a woman?

It was a little disturbing that neither of them felt any urgent desire to make the final jump, perhaps because they were both so comfortable as they were.

If they did marry, Fiona would have to sell her flat and move into his Georgian house close to Regent's Park, in which he had lived all his life, his father having inherited it from his own father, old James Ormond the first, who had founded the firm and bought the house in 1895. James couldn't imagine living anywhere else. If he felt passion for anything it was for his home. He loved every brick of it, every painting, piece of furniture, even every blade of grass in the garden.

Thirty-five, and very settled in his ways, he did not want his well-run life to change. He expected it to go on in just the same way for ever, even if he married and had children. He wanted children; he would like a son

to inherit the business in turn, one day, and then maybe
Fiona would want a daughter after that, but neither of
them would want a large family. The children and the
home would be Fiona's province. She would get a
nanny, of course, and continue to work, at least part-
time. She was an only child, too, and would inherit her
family business, but she liked to make decisions and be
in charge; she would enjoy taking care of their home
and family.

Yes, he was sure they would build a good life together, but there was plenty of time. No hurry.

The telephone on his desk rang again and he swung
back to pick it up, saying curtly, 'I thought I told you I
didn't want interruptions? I hope this is urgent.'

'I'm sorry, Mr Ormond, but Miss Kirby has rung
again and insists on speaking to you. This is the fourth
time she's rung; I can't get rid of her.'

'Have you found out who she is? Has she told you
what she wants to speak to me about?'

Miss Roper's voice was expressionless and discreet.
'She says she wants to talk to you about your mother,
sir.'

James stiffened, his face losing all its colour, turning
pale and immobile.

There was half a moment of silence. He heard his
wristwatch ticking, a pigeon cooing on the windowsill
outside, and from the river the sigh of a spring wind.

His voice harsh, he said at last, 'My mother is dead;
you know that perfectly well! I don't know what she's
up to, but I do not want to speak to her, now or ever.
Hang up, and then tell the switchboard not to put through
any more calls from Miss Kirby.'

Dropping the phone back on its rest, he leaned back

in his chair, his hands flat on the leather top of the desk, grey eyes bleak as they stared straight ahead.

His tie was too tightly tied; he couldn't breathe. He angrily loosened the knot, undid the top button of his shirt.

Nobody had mentioned his mother to him since he was ten years old and she had vanished from his life for ever. He hadn't even thought of her for years. He didn't want to think about her now.

What was this Kirby woman up to? Was this some sort of blackmail attempt? Maybe he should have got Miss Roper to call the police? Or the security firm he employed to check on dubious clients? He could easily find out everything he needed to know about this Kirby woman, from where she had been born to whether or not she took sugar in her tea. But why waste time and money? She couldn't be any sort of problem to him.

Oh, no? Women can always be a problem, he thought grimly. Even someone as rational and sensible as Fiona did crazy things, like eating cheese when she knew it gave her migraine. Miss Roper was prepared to annoy him in spite of the very high salary he paid her, simply because she had a mother living at home when she could easily find her a nice, comfortable nursing home where she would be well taken care of day and night. Women might have good brains, might try to think calmly and reasonably, but they usually ended up thinking with their hearts instead of their heads.

His mouth was oddly dry; he needed a drink. Getting up, he walked over to a discreetly concealed cabinet in the oak-panelled wall.

Opening it, James selected a tumbler and poured himself a finger of good malt whisky, dropped ice cubes into the glass and shut the cabinet again, then walked back to his desk, nursing his whisky.

He rarely drank before the evening, apart from a glass or two of wine during lunch. He sat down, leaned back, sipping the whisky. He must put the whole stupid incident out of his mind and get on with his work.

He looked at his watch. Half an hour left; he might still finish the report before he had to meet Charles, if he wasn't interrupted again. Finishing his drink, he turned his attention back to the closely typed pages.

He was on the final page when a confused noise began outside. James looked up, frowning. Now what?

Someone was shouting—it was Miss Roper's voice, he recognised a second later with amazement, since he had never heard her shout that way before.

'No, he doesn't want to see you! Look, I'm sorry… You can't go in there! Stop…'

The door fell open and bodies crashed through into his office. Three bodies, to be precise. Miss Roper. Her halfwitted assistant. And a third woman, who rolled across the floor in a flurry of arms and legs and fiery red hair in a tangle of tight, exploding curls, finishing up close to him.

James was so stunned that he didn't even move; he just sat there behind his desk, staring down at her.

Clutching at a chair to stop herself falling, Miss Roper burst into stammering explanation, on the verge of tears.

'I told her…said she couldn't…she forced her way past me. I'm sorry, I did my best…she wouldn't listen.'

Her assistant was already backing out, away from James's terrifying presence, making gasping noises of panic and alarm. He took no notice of her, expecting nothing else from her by now, and in any case far too intent on the third person who had imploded into his room.

She was at his feet, quite literally, suddenly reaching out and attaching herself to his shoes with both hands, clinging on like a limpet.

'I'm not going until you let me talk to you!'

James looked at Miss Roper again. 'Is this who I think it is? The Kirby woman?'

'Patience Kirby,' said the girl, her slanty hazel eyes fixed on his face. 'Please, Mr Ormond, just give me five minutes of your time, that's all I ask. I won't go until you do.'

'Call Security, Miss Roper,' James ordered, flinty-hearted.

Miss Roper gulped and headed for her own office.

'You might as well get up,' James told the girl. 'I am not listening to you. If you aren't out of here in one minute my security men will carry you out. And let go of my feet!' He couldn't move with her tethered to him, except by dragging her along with him.

Her hands let go of his shoes, but she immediately shot up and clasped his legs instead, wrapping her arms around them. 'Why won't you listen to me?'

'You tiresome female! Let go of me, will you? You're making yourself ridiculous—this isn't some soap on TV; this is real life and you are in serious trouble. I could have you arrested for forcing an entry and physical assault!'

'I've got a message from your mother,' she said, ignoring his threats.

'My mother is dead!' James heard the running feet of the security men along the stone floors in the corridor from the lift. Thank God, they would be here soon to end this embarrassing scene.

'No, she isn't, she's alive.' She bit her lip, frowning. 'You didn't really think she was dead, did you?' The small face lifted to him had an annoyingly childlike look: heart-shaped, with large, beautifully spaced glowing eyes fringed by a ludicrous number of thick ginger lashes which shone in the sunlight like gold, a small nose and a wide, warm mouth. She wasn't pretty, but she was oddly appealing. Not his type, of course; he preferred women to be elegant and coolly beautiful, with good brains, like Fiona, but he could imagine that boys of her own age might find this girl adorable.

'My mother is dead!' he insisted, his teeth snapping out the words.

'Did your father tell you that? And all this time you've believed she was…? Oh, that's terrible.' Tears actually formed in those eyes. One began sliding down her cheek while James watched it incredulously.

'Stop that!' he muttered. 'What are you crying about?'

'It's so sad…when I think of you… How could your father lie to you like that? Only ten years old, to be told your mother was dead! You must have been heartbroken.'

He had been. He remembered the coldness that had sunk into him, the misery and anguish, the sense of betrayal, of desertion. Of course, his father hadn't told him his mother was dead. His father wasn't a man given to telling lies. He had told him the cold, bitter truth.

'Your mother has run off with another man and left us both,' his father had said curtly. 'You'll never see her again.'

James had been taken off to stay with an aunt who had a bungalow at Greatstone, on the Kent coast, and had stood, day after day, on the beach, staring out at the grey, heaving waters of the English Channel, listening to the melancholy cry of gulls, the slow, sad whisper of the tide rising and falling on the sand. Whenever he heard those sounds something inside him ached, a stupid emotional echo of almost forgotten pain.

'But she isn't dead! She's alive!' said Patience Kirby.

'She's dead to me,' James said tersely.

It was too late now for his mother to come back. He had spent a quarter of a century living without her; he had no need of a mother now.

Three security men burst into the room, big men in dark uniforms and peaked caps, ready to do battle with whatever they might find.

'Get her away from me,' James ordered.

The girl turned her small, heart-shaped face to them. They stared at her tear-wet eyes and trembling lips, then all three men shuffled their feet and looked sheepish.

One of them said uneasily, 'Better get up, miss.'

Another offered her a hand. 'Come on, miss, let me help you up.'

'No, I'm not moving!' she obstinately refused, shaking her head so that the red curls flew around like the petals of a flower in wind.

'Well, don't just stand there, pick her up!' ordered James, and leaned down to loosen her grip on his legs.

Her hands were smaller than he had expected; soft little fingers curled around his like tendrils of vine around a tree and he felt a queer tremor in his chest. Clutching them, he stood up, pulling her up with him. She came without a struggle, her head just below his shoulder level.

Was she an adult, or a child pretending to be grown up? he wondered, looking down at her in closer, sharper assessment. Five foot two or three, and, no, not a child, just a very small girl in her early twenties, in scruffy blue jeans and a cheap dark blue cotton sweatshirt which clung to small breasts and a skinny waist. Yet she was not boyish; indeed she was amazingly female in a way he found hard to explain to himself.

'Your mother's alive, Mr Ormond,' she said softly. 'She's old and broke, and lonely. It would make her so happy to see you. She's all alone in the world and she needs you.'

'You mean she needs money,' he said with a cynical twist of his lips. Now and then he wondered if his mother would one day get in touch and ask for money; he had never been quite sure whether or not he would give her any. In the divorce settlement she had been given a pretty considerable sum, his father had assured him; she was not entitled to anything else. But she had always been extravagant, his father had said; she would probably run through her money and be back for more one day.

Patience Kirby bit her lip. 'Well, she hasn't much, it's true—just her old-age pension, actually, and when she has paid her rent she has barely enough to live on—but I throw in three meals a day and...'

'You throw in three meals a day?' he interrupted sharply.

'She's living with me.'

My God, is this girl her child? His stomach sank. He hated the idea. Is this my half-sister, daughter of whatever man his mother had run off with twenty-five years ago? He searched her face, looking for some resemblance, but found none. The girl did not look like his mother or any of their family.

'I run a little hotel, a sort of boarding-house,' Patience Kirby said. 'The local Social Services people send me old people who need somewhere cheap to live. That's how I got your mother; she came three months ago. She's very frail; she'll only be sixty next week, but she looks much older, she's had such a hard life. She's been living abroad, in France and Italy, singing in hotels and bars, she told me. Earning very little, just enough to keep her going.

'I thought she had nobody in the world, then one day she told me about you, said she hadn't seen you since you were ten. She thinks about you all the time; she has pictures of you and cuttings from newspapers about you stuck up everywhere around her room. She would give anything to see you at least once. You're all she has in the world now, and she's sick; the doctor doesn't think she'll live for more than a couple of years.'

James was furiously aware of their audience—the three security men, Miss Roper, the bird-brained assistant—all standing on the other side of the room, listening with obvious sympathy, their eyes moving from the girl's emotional face to his set, cold one, their expressions reproaching him for being so hard-hearted.

Harshly, he said, 'My mother chose to go away with some man twenty-five years ago, leaving me and my father without a backward look. It's too late now for her to turn up and ask for help, but if you leave your name and address with my secretary I'll make arrangements for her to start receiving some sort of pension.'

'That isn't what she wants!' Patience Kirby burst out. 'She wants to see *you*!'

'But I don't want to see her! Now, I'm very busy, I have a lunch appointment and I am going out.'

'I'm not leaving here until you promise to come and see her, at least once!'

James told the security men, through clenched teeth, 'Get her out of here, will you?'

They shuffled forward. 'Please come along, miss!'

She sat down in James's chair, hazel eyes defiant, red hair tumbling over her small face, and held on tightly to the arms. 'I am staying put!'

Helplessly, they looked at their employer.

'Pick her up and carry her out!' James snarled. 'Unless you no longer want your jobs?'

Galvanised by this threat, the three took reluctant hold of Patience Kirby's arms and legs, in spite of her struggles, and began to carry her towards the door.

'How can you be so heartless? Whatever she did all those years ago, she's still your mother!'

'She should have remembered that fact years ago. Now, don't come back or next time you're going out of the window!' he shouted after her disappearing red curls, surprised to hear his own voice sounding so out of control.

He hated losing control; it was Patience Kirby's fault; she had pushed him to the limit. But she had wasted her time. He was going to forget everything she had said about his mother; you didn't wipe out a lifetime of rejection by simply turning up and asking for forgiveness after twenty-five years. Patience Kirby wasn't getting through his defences a second time. He would see to that. He hoped never to set eyes on the girl again.

CHAPTER TWO

As HE left the office shortly afterwards James told Miss Roper to find out how Patience Kirby had got up to his floor and make sure it did not happen again.

'She should never have got past the receptionist, let alone into a lift. Check which receptionist was working this morning, and which security guard was on duty by the lifts. That girl could have been a terrorist or a bank robber! Security has obviously become very lax. I want them to have a surprise security exercise tomorrow. Let's see how alert the team really is!'

'Yes, sir.' Miss Roper sounded meek enough but James knew her very well; she rarely called him sir, and when she did it was always a sign of suppressed rage over something that had upset her. He could see that her normally placid brown eyes were smouldering, glinting with red. Miss Roper was angry with him; she hadn't approved of the way he'd dealt with Patience Kirby. She didn't understand how he felt. Miss Roper's mother hadn't left her when she was ten years old.

'Don't look at me like that!' he crossly said, then turned away and stamped off to the lift feeling ill-treated and sorry for himself.

His chauffeur, Barny King, always drove him during the day so that James did not have to hunt for a parking space. Barny would drop him wherever he wanted to go, then drive off back to Regent's Park, have his own lunch with his wife, Enid, in the kitchen of James's house, and when James summoned him by telephone drive back to pick him up again.

He would be waiting outside now; he was always punctual. You could rely on Barny and he wouldn't dream of implying criticism. Only women thought they had a God-given right to sit in judgement on other people. Men were far more reasonable and tolerant.

James did not use the same lift as all the other bank employees; he had an express lift which shot you straight down to the ground floor or the underground car park without stopping on any of the other seventeen floors. His father had installed it not long before he died because he'd feared being buttonholed with complaints or requests for a rise by employees using the opportunity of being in the same lift.

Emerging on the marble-tiled ground floor, James paused to glance around in case Patience Kirby was hanging about, but he didn't see her. There were crowds going in and out of the other lifts, walking to the revolving doors which led to the busy city street, taking the escalator upwards. But no Patience.

What a name for a little hothead like her! Her parents must have seen that red hair and expected her to have a temper to match, surely! The name must have been their warped idea of a joke.

As he walked across the foyer James admired the decor, as he always did; he had chosen the design of the long, high, wide plate glass wall along one side, admitting as much light as possible, the marble-tiled floors and the glass-walled escalator which slowly ascended through hanging vines and rubber plants which were of a tropical height now and kept on climbing. The original bank had been a far darker place, with fewer, smaller windows and no plants at all, just ancient, creaky, over-fussy furniture.

As a child he had not enjoyed his visits; he had thought the place gloomy and alarming, and had not looked forward to working there, as he knew his father would insist he did when he was old enough.

Looking back down the long tunnel of those years, he couldn't remember what he would have liked to do instead. Drive a train, maybe? Or be an explorer? He certainly had not wanted to work in a bank. It was his destiny, his father had told him. Doom would have been a more accurate word.

When his father died, four years ago, James's first act as managing director and chairman had been to begin making changes to the structure of the bank in an effort to create a more pleasant working environment for the staff and customers. The work had cost millions, but every time he looked around the light-filled reception area, the glass and greenery, he was satisfied that it had been well worth it.

The dark and gloomy building he remembered from his childhood had been buried for ever in his memory.

He hurried out through the revolving doors and across the pavement to where his chauffeur was holding open the door of the white Daimler. James shot into the back and gave a sigh of relief as Barny closed the door on him and walked round to get behind the wheel.

'Lock the doors!' James ordered, and with a glance of surprise Barny obeyed.

'Something wrong, Mr James?'

'No, just taking precautions,' James enigmatically said, deciding not to mention Patience Kirby's visit.

A man in his mid-fifties, with iron-grey hair sliding back from his forehead, leaving his scalp shiny and smooth, Barny King had been working for the Ormond family for years. He had driven James to boarding school, aged ten, with a set, pale face and very cold hands, had ferried him and all his luggage to Cambridge when he went off to university, trying to look thirty when he was actually only eighteen, and he had driven old Mr Ormond back and forth to the City from the exquisite house in Regent's Park, where Barny and his wife had a private apartment over the garage.

Barny and Enid were an important part of James's life, as important to him as Miss Roper but even closer because they had known him as a child and been kind to him when he needed kindness, comforting when he was lonely. When he remembered his childhood from the age of ten he remembered Barny and Enid, rarely his father. They had almost been parents to him; he had happy memories of sitting in the kitchen with them eating buttered crumpets and home-made jam sandwiches, neither of which were permitted on the table if he ate with his father.

James stared out of the window as they drove off. Patience Kirby must have given up and gone away. He suddenly remembered those tiny, soft warm hands clutching at him and felt a strange stab of undefined feeling in his chest.

Angry with himself, he frowned, pushed the memory of her away, got the financial report out of his briefcase and began skimming it through again. He wanted all the details fresh in his mind when he met Charles.

Traffic along Piccadilly was as heavy as usual, but Barny fought his way through to drop James at the side entrance of the Ritz.

'I'll ring for you in a couple of hours,' James told him, getting out.

He found Charles in the Palm Court, drinking a champagne cocktail. Waving cheerfully, Charles summoned the waiter to bring another for James.

'Lovely day, isn't it?'

James looked blank. 'Is it? I hadn't noticed.'

Charles roared with laughter. 'All work and no play, Jimmy.'

He had always called him Jimmy, indifferent to the fact that James hated it. James sipped his cocktail and studied the menu, choosing in the end to have rocket and anchovy salad sprinkled with grated parmesan followed by a Dover sole with asparagus and new potatoes.

'Grilled, served off the bone,' he instructed, and the head waiter nodded.

'Yes, sir.'

'Sometimes I get *déjà vu*, lunching with you, Jimmy,' Charles said. 'You're the image of your old dad. Time whizzes back for me, listening to you.'

'I'm flattered,' James said, knowing Charles had not intended to flatter him, was being sarcastic. 'I was very attached to my father.'

Charles made a face. 'Really? I hated mine. Never stopped lecturing me, tedious old Victorian of a chap.'

They ate in the beautiful dining room looking over Green Park. Their table was in a corner by the windows, which were slightly open to let mild spring air into the room, setting the gilded metal chains on the elaborately painted ceiling swinging and tinkling softly.

They talked business throughout the meal, but occasionally James looked out into the park at the daffodils, golden and swaying, under the trees which were just breaking into tiny, bright green leaf.

Noticing his occasional abstraction, Charles grinned at him. 'How's Fiona, Jimmy?'

How James hated that nickname, but he suppressed a shudder. 'She's fine, thanks.'

'Ravishing girl, you lucky boy! I'd swap places with you any day. You've been seeing her for months, haven't you? We going to hear the ringing of wedding bells before long?'

James gave him a cool look. Charles was not that close a friend and James had no intention of discussing Fiona or his personal life with him.

When he didn't answer, Charles said cynically, 'In no hurry to tie yourself down, eh? I wish I'd been as wise as you. Well, I've learnt my lesson now. No more marriages for me. In future I'll just have affairs.'

In his early fifties, elegant, willowy, always smoothly tailored, with silvering at his temples among the smooth raven-black hair, Charles had been married four times so far and was currently in the middle of his latest divorce from a much younger woman, a ravishing TV star with her own series.

Coming home late after a business dinner, Charles had caught her in bed with her co-star. He might not have minded so much if it had not been the matrimonial bed, his own bed in his own bedroom, and if the other man had not been her age and something of a sexual athlete.

The divorce was to have been discreet, on grounds of breakdown of the marriage. Charles had not wanted the whole world to know his wife had been cheating on him with a much younger man. But his wife had not been so silent; she had given exclusive interviews to several daily newspapers and Charles had had the chagrin of reading intimate details of his sex life printed for everyone to see.

As they began to eat, James produced the report he had spent the morning studying and asked a series of shrewd questions. Charles might be a fool where women were concerned but he had a good business mind and was able to tell James everything he needed to know.

The bottle of good white wine they were drinking had vanished long before they finished their main course, but James had consumed very little of it. He disliked drinking too much over lunch; it always meant you got very little done during the rest of the day.

He refused a pudding, ordering a pot of coffee; Charles, however, asked for spotted dick with custard and ate it when it came with half-closed, delighted eyes.

'Delicious, just like school pud. You should have had some.'

'I never eat puddings, especially heavy ones.'

'Puritan! Your problem is you were never taught to enjoy life. That gloomy old father of yours had a very bad influence on you.'

James could have said that his father had taught him not to keep marrying women who cost a fortune and were always unfaithful, not to drink like a fish and wake up late every morning with a hangover, and not to spend his days hanging around bars and going to wild parties. But where was the point in offending Charles by telling him the truth?

He looked at his watch. 'Sorry, Charles, I have to rush off. I have an appointment at three. Thanks for all your help.' He pulled his mobile out of his briefcase and called Barny, told him to come at once, then called the waiter over, asked for the bill, signed it, dropped a tip on the plate and stood up.

'I think I'll have a little brandy before I go,' Charles said, settling comfortably in his chair. 'Thanks for lunch, old boy. My love to Fiona. Sexy as hell, you lucky bastard.'

James went to the cloakroom, used the lavatory, washed his face and hands and brushed his black hair back, staring at himself in the mirror. His grey eyes had a wintry look. Would he call Fiona sexy? Not a word he would have chosen to describe her, no. Beautiful, yes. Elegant, yes. But sexy? No, she was far too cold.

A shiver ran down his spine. Was that what he really thought about her? Dismay filled him. Of course she wasn't cold. Cool, maybe, but not cold.

Yet the grey eyes reflected in the mirror had a distinctly uneasy look. This was being a very unsettling day so far. He hurriedly turned from the mirror, collected his coat, shrugged into it, tipped the cloakroom attendant and went out of the hotel to find Barny just pulling up outside.

'I hope I didn't keep you waiting, Mr James. Traffic a bit heavy the other side of the park today.'

James smiled at him. 'No, I just left the hotel. Perfect timing, Barny, as always. Back to the office, now. Did Enid give you a good lunch?'

'Her oxtail stew and mashed potatoes, and then I had an apple.'

'Lucky Barny. One of my favourites. What is she making tonight?'

'Thought you were going out for dinner this evening, sir.' Barny looked anxiously into the driving mirror. 'We booked to see the new musical, Mr James—will you need us, after all?'

'No, no, I'd forgotten. Of course I'm eating out.' James did not want to ruin their evening just because his own had been cancelled. He might as well still eat at the new restaurant as he had a table booked.

Barny relaxed with a barely audible sigh of relief. 'You had me worried there—Enid is really looking for-

ward to seeing this show. You know how she loves a
good musical. She's such a romantic, my Enid.'

Eyes warming, James smiled back at him. 'Always
was, I remember. How many Sunday afternoons did I
spend with Enid watching weepie films on TV, feeding
her paper tissues to mop her eyes with? Well, have a
lovely evening. Could you pick me up at five and drop
me at my club? Then you'll be free. I'll get a taxi back
home tonight.'

'Right, Mr James, thanks.' Barny drew up outside the
bank; James looked around hurriedly before getting out,
but there was still no sign of Patience Kirby's bright red
head. He felt a queer little niggle inside his chest; he
told himself it was relief. She was the last thing he
wanted to see. Crazy girl. But he was surprised—had
she really given up and gone home?

He had a much busier afternoon and hardly had time
to think about anything except work. At five o'clock
precisely he went down in his lift and walked out of the
bank to where Barny was waiting.

By then he had forgotten Patience Kirby. He got into
the back of the Daimler; Barny walked round to get into
the driver's seat. The window beside James was half-
open. A little hand came through it suddenly and
grabbed his shoulder. Startled, he looked out into those
large, luminous hazel eyes. Stupidly, for a second all he
could think about was the tiny golden flecks around her
dark pupil, like rays of sunlight fading into the soft hazel
iris.

'Won't you please change your mind? Surely you
could spare an hour to drive over and see her? Just once,
that isn't too much to ask, is it? If you could only see
how frail she is, you wouldn't refuse. She looks as if a
breath of wind would blow her away.'

'Can't you understand English? As far as I'm concerned she's dead. I'm not interested in renewing our acquaintance. Now, let go of me, will you? Drive on, Barny!'

He was hot with temper, partly because for a second he had felt his heart lift as if with delight, and that was disturbing, and partly because some of his employees were coming out of the bank, shamelessly eavesdropping and staring. This would be all round the bank tomorrow morning. In all his time at the bank James had never been the centre of scandal and he was furious at the prospect of all the gossip he could be sure would follow.

'How can you be so hard-hearted?' Patience Kirby hurled at him, her eyes glittering. 'Your own mother!'

James heard an intake of breath from Barny, felt him swivel in his seat to stare with clearly shocked eyes. Damn her! What was she going to do next? Ring the national newspapers and give them the story, spread it right across the country?

'I'm going to shut this window; get your hand out of it!' he muttered, his hand reaching for the button.

The window began to slide upward. She snatched her hand away only at the last moment.

'Drive off, Barny!' snapped James.

Barny automatically obeyed, accelerating away fast just as James realised that the window had shut on Patience Kirby's sleeve. To his horror he also realised that she was being dragged along with the car, her red hair blowing around the pale, frightened face he could still see outside his window.

'Stop! For God's sake, stop!' he yelled at Barny, who slammed on his brakes. The Daimler came to a shuddering halt.

It was at that point that James made a stupid, over-hasty move. He operated the electric switch, the window slid down, releasing her sleeve, and the red hair disappeared from his view. It was only at that second that he realised he should have waited, got out on the other side of the car and held her while Barny opened the window. As it was, she tumbled to the pavement with a crash that made his heart crash in echo. Jumping out, he found her lying face down; he hurriedly knelt down beside her, white-faced in shock. By then a crowd was beginning to gather, staring with a mixture of curiosity and hostility.

'What's happened?' one woman asked another, who shrugged.

'Think he knocked her down.'

'Poor girl! Looks bad to me. Dead, I'd say.'

Barny had got out too. 'How is she, sir?' he asked, and James noted the slight frost in his tone and knew Barny was now as disapproving as Miss Roper. What was happening to everyone in his life? They were all starting to look at him as if he was a monster.

He had a strange suspicion that if he looked in a mirror right now he would find his own eyes held a similar expression.

Patience Kirby sat up shakily. 'Are you okay?' James asked. 'You'd better not move until we get an ambulance.'

She put a hand to her head; James saw blood on both.

'You're bleeding! Barny, ring for an ambulance!'

Patience Kirby hurriedly staggered to her feet, using James's arm for support.

'No, really, I don't want to go to hospital. They are bound to be busy. It will mean spending hours in Casualty waiting to be seen and all that's wrong with me is a few cuts and bruises.'

'You don't know that! You could have some broken bones.'

She flexed a slim ankle, took a couple of swaying steps. 'See, I can walk; I haven't broken anything.'

'What about your head? That hit the pavement with an almighty crack.'

'Oh, I've got a tough skull.' But she did not seem to James to be too steady on her feet, all the same.

'Was she trying to snatch something out of your car?' a man in the crowd hissed next to him. 'I saw her grabbing at you through the window. Don't know what the City's coming to, street girls hanging about in broad daylight! You expect them up West, but not around here. You be careful, mister, I don't think she's hurt at all— just a bit of blackmail. I'll be a witness for you if the cops come. I saw it was an accident; don't you let her trap you.'

James gave him such a ferocious sideways glance that the man backed off hurriedly, muttering. 'Oh, well, if you want to make a fool of yourself, don't let me stop you.'

'You should be X-rayed to make sure there are no fractures,' James told Patience, who shook her head, grimacing.

'I hate hospitals.'

'Nevertheless it's only sensible...'

'I won't go, okay? Look, if I feel any worse tomorrow I'll go along to Casualty. Please stop fussing. You're worse than my grandpa.'

Being compared to her grandfather went down like a lead balloon with James. Tight-lipped, he said, 'Get in the car, please. I'll give you a lift home.'

The crowd began to disperse, seeing that no further excitement was likely.

Her hazel eyes glinted mischievously up at him. 'Remember, I might pick your pocket if you let me get close enough.'

'Very droll, Miss Kirby. Please get into the car.'

She obeyed this time, but was still looking up at him, which was why she stumbled over the edge of the kerb.

Before she could hit her chin on the open car door James grabbed her, slid an arm around her waist, another behind her knees, and carried her to the car, very conscious of her glinting red hair brushing his jawline, her heart beating under that shabby old sweatshirt she wore, picking up a faint, flowery scent from her throat. If you missed the slight rise of those tiny breasts you'd think she could be a boy, she was so slightly built, so skinny of hip and leg, but it would be a mistake to forget her femininity. He had already been stung by it once or twice. Looking at her was one thing; having her in his arms made an entirely different and disturbing impression.

She looked like a child, but she got her own way with a woman's maddening deviance. He had been determined not to visit her home and here he was, committed to doing just that—and the really infuriating part was that he didn't even really mind.

Not that he was really attracted to a skinny brat like this, of course! Good God, no! It was just that... He tried to explain his reactions to himself, to be rational and level-headed, but she had slid her arms round his neck and put her head on his shoulder and James was suddenly having some sort of problem thinking at all.

Almost feverishly he deposited her in a hurry on the back seat of the car and climbed in beside her, trying not to make his agitation visible.

What the hell was the matter with him? He was behaving like some sex-starved lunatic.

Slamming the door, he watched Barny get back behind his driving wheel. Without looking at the girl,
James asked curtly, 'What's the address?'

'Muswell Hill, Cheney Road; the house is called The
Cedars.'

The address intrigued him; it sounded Victorian, gracious, and didn't fit this girl at all. He would be curious
to see what her home looked like, what sort of family
she came from. But he wouldn't go into the house; he
was not letting her win every trick. He would drop her
and drive away.

'Make for Muswell Hill, Barney,' James said, leaning
forward to open a small cabinet fixed to the back of the
front seats. It held among other things first aid items;
James selected a box of paper handkerchiefs, a bottle of
still water and a couple of sticky plasters.

'Turn your face to me, Miss Kirby.'

'Patience,' she said, obeying.

'That's a very old-fashioned name.'

'My aunt's; she was rich and my parents hoped she
would leave me her money if they called me by her
name.'

'Did she?'

'No, she left it to a cat's home. In her will she said
she had always hated her name, and if my parents hadn't
called me Patience she would have left me her money,
but she despised them for saddling an innocent child
with a name like that and said money had never helped
her enjoy life so I'd be better off without any.'

James laughed. 'She sounds interesting. And were
you?'

'Was I what?'

'Better off without her money.'

Sadly she shook her head.

He began cleaning the blood from her forehead, exposing a long but thankfully merely a surface cut. James washed and dried·it before covering it with a plaster, then washed the rest of her heart-shaped face and dried it carefully, very aware of her looking up at him, curling dark gold lashes deepening the effect of those eyes. He wished she would stop staring. Uneasiness made him brusque. 'Head hurting much?'

'Not at all.'

He held up three fingers. 'How many fingers can you see?'

'Three, of course.'

He stared into the centres of the hazel eyes but the pupils seemed normal, neither dilated nor contracted. She smiled, a sweet, warm curve of the mouth that made him flush for some inexplicable reason.

He scowled. No, that wasn't honest; he knew very well why he had gone red. He had wanted to kiss that warm, wide mouth. He still did; in fact just contemplating the possibility made him dizzy. I'm light-headed, he thought. Am I coming down with some bug? There is flu going around the office. That must be it. Why would I want to kiss her? I don't even like this girl; she's a nuisance. She isn't much to look at, either. Not my type.

She's too young for you, anyway, a little voice inside his head insisted. Look at her! You can give her a good fifteen years.

Don't exaggerate! he told himself. Ten, maybe—she's in her early twenties, not her teens!

She had been watching him, now she looked down, her dark gold lashes stirring against her cheeks. James hoped she hadn't picked up what was in his mind. He didn't want her getting any crazy ideas about his intentions. As far as she was concerned, he did not have any!

A moment later Barny slowed, turning a corner. 'This is the road; where exactly do I find the house, miss?' He and James both contemplated the road of detached houses in large gardens. It certainly matched the address the girl had given them, but it did not match the girl herself. She didn't look as if she came from one of these gracious period homes set among trees and shrubs, with curving drives, and lawns.

'Keep driving and I'll tell you when to stop,' Patience said, and obediently Barny kerb-crawled until she said, 'This is it!'

The car stopped outside and both men stared curiously at the high Victorian house with gabled pink roofs on several levels, twisty red barley sugar chimneys, latticed windows behind which hung pretty chintz curtains. Built of red brick, the woodwork painted apple-green, the design made it look more like a cottage than a large house, a typical design of the last quarter of the nineteenth century. It was set well back from the road in large gardens in which spring was busy breaking out.

A flurry of almond blossom on black boughs, green lawns covered in daisies, yellow trumpets of daffodils and purple crocus showing in naturalised clumps— James hadn't noticed until now how far spring had progressed. There was an over-civilised tidiness to his own garden that missed out on this lyrical note.

'The Cedars?' he queried drily. 'What happened to them?'

'There is one, but it's at the back. There were two when the house was built; the other one blew down in a storm years ago.' She gave him a defiant glare. 'And will you stop being sarcastic?'

He didn't answer. 'Barny, take us up to the front door.'

Barny swung the car through the green-painted open gates and slowly drove up to the porch which sheltered a verandah and a green front door. He stopped right outside; James got out of the car and turned to help Patience out.

'Here you are. Goodbye. And I don't want to see you again.'

She slid down from the car and stumbled over his foot. Quite deliberately, in his opinion, but it would be useless to point that out. Sighing, James caught her before she hit the path and picked her up. She was beginning to feel comfortable in his arms. He would have to watch that. This girl was insidious as ivy; she would be growing all over him soon if he wasn't careful.

'Okay, this is the last thing I do,' he told her coldly. 'I will carry you to your front door, but I am not going inside.'

He waited for an argument, but didn't get one, which was ominous in itself. He would dump her on the doorstep and run back to the car and safety.

She looked over his shoulder at Barny, gave him that lovely, sweet smile. 'Thank you, Barny.'

Suspiciously, James demanded, 'How do you know his name?'

She turned her hazel eyes up to him. 'You've been calling him that all the way.'

He got the smile this time, and felt his stomach muscles contract disturbingly.

'You are funny,' she told him indulgently.

He carried her up the steps on to the verandah and over the painted wooden floor which creaked every step of the way. James forced himself to put her down at the front door.

'Well, goodbye, Miss Kirby, don't come to my office again. I have tightened up security procedures; you won't get in again.'

She gave him a distinctly wicked glance through her long, darkened lashes. 'I bet I could if I really tried.'

He bet she could, too. His security men were only human.

Sternly, he said, 'Don't try. I would hate you to land in jail.'

'You'd love it,' she said, mouth curling, pink and teasing. 'Men love to exercise power. Tyranny is their favourite occupation.'

James refused to argue with her any more. He turned to go back to the car, but at that second the front door swung open and a noisy multitude rushed out of the house and engulfed him in barking dogs with wagging tails and licking tongues, what appeared to be a dozen yelling children in scruffy jeans and sweaters, two old ladies in floral aprons and an old man in dirty boots and dungarees.

James should have fled there and then but he was too slow, too busy looking at the old ladies and wondering if one of them was his mother. He saw no resemblance at all, but then would he, after twenty-five years? Patience had said that his mother was frail and delicate. The description did not fit either of the two women; they looked tough and capable, in spite of both being at least seventy years old.

'He's taken our puppy and he's going to drown it!' one of the children sobbed. 'Make him give it back.'

Patience was greeting dogs, her small hands busy on their heads, impeded by their licking tongues. 'What puppy?' she asked the tallest child, a boy with a mop of familiar red hair and eyes like melting toffee.

The old man answered her gruffly. 'They found it and brought it home with them. As if there weren't enough dogs underfoot without bringing puppies back here!'

'I found it,' the smallest child said, a little boy with spiky ginger hair. 'I bringed it home in my spaceship.'

'Spaceship?' asked Patience.

'Her wheelbarrow,' interpreted the eldest boy.

Her wheelbarrow? That was a girl?

Patience smiled down at the smallest child, ruffling the hedgehog-like hair.

'Where did you find it, Emmy? It must belong to someone! They'll be worried about it; we must let them know the puppy is safe.'

'No good,' the old man grunted. 'They don't want it back. They're not daft; they jumped at the chance to get rid of it.'

'The lady at Wayside House gave it to me!' said Emmy. 'She said nobody wanted it and I could have it, and it likes me. It wanted to come with me, it licked my face and jumped in my spaceship, but Joe says he's going to drown it. Don't let him, Patience, please...'

Emmy began to cry, tears seeping out of her eyes as if she was melting, and trickling down her small face.

'This place is already overrun with animals; we've got to take a stand!'

'I hate you, I hate you,' Emmy sobbed, and kicked the old man with surprising violence on his ankle.

He hopped back. 'Here, you stop that!'

As if at a given signal, the children all surged forward and were clearly about to launch a physical attack on him, too, but Patience said sharply, 'No! Don't be naughty, children!' and they fell back obediently but glared and muttered.

'He's a nasty man!' Emmy said, still dripping tears.

'And what business is it of his, anyway?' the tallest boy said, his voice breaking with temper, making him sound oddly touching, stranded halfway between child and man, neither one nor the other.

Patience produced a handkerchief and gently wiped Emmy's wet little face. 'You shouldn't kick grown-ups; you know that, Emmy.'

'Not even if they deserve it?' the tall boy asked cuttingly.

Patience looked confused. 'Not even then, Toby,' she said at last, and the children shifted, scowling.

By then James had worked out that there weren't actually a dozen, only about half a dozen, and he wasn't sure if they were all related. The ones with hair on the red side were probably related to Patience; the three others of about the same ages were probably just their friends.

Barny got out of the car and came up the steps, asking quietly, 'Are you coming, sir? I have to get back to Enid, if you remember, or we'll be late for the theatre.'

Patience swivelled to look at James; the children, the old women and the old man all stared, too, silenced for a second or two and taking James in then, their eyes curious, probing. 'Is it him?' the children whispered to Patience, who nodded at them, putting a finger on her lips.

James knew he should be going. This whole family were obviously crazy. Nothing like this had ever happened to him before. His life had always been so neat and ordered, a world of calm colours and hushed voices. He couldn't help being fascinated by this revelation of

a very different universe and he hesitated, feeling he
should leave yet so curious he knew he would stay.

'Off you go, Barny, you mustn't keep Enid waiting.
I'll get a taxi,' he said offhandedly.

Barny nodded. 'Yes, sir.' For some reason he smiled,
too, as if he was pleased with James, although why he
should be James could not imagine, flushing slightly and
feeling irritated and self-conscious. Barny went back
down the steps; the car drove off and James felt one last
wild urge to run after it, but at that instant a tiny hand
twined itself around his fingers.

He looked down into the bright green eyes of the little
girl.

'Come and see my puppy. Do you like puppies?'

'Don't encourage her,' said the old man. 'You can see
how many dogs we've got. The last thing we need is
another dog, and this puppy isn't even house-trained; it
leaves puddles everywhere and it has already torn up a
cushion and Mrs Green's slipper—chewed it to bits, it
did.'

'Oh, never mind that old slipper! I don't care twopence about it. Don't you drown that poor little mite on
my account!' said a spry, white-haired woman whose
blue flowered apron exactly matched her blue eyes. 'I'll
soon house-train him. I've always had a soft spot for a
Jack Russell, and he'll certainly keep the vermin down.
We won't need to worry about rats or mice if we have
that little chap here.'

'Oh, that's it! Undermine my authority!' scolded the
old man.

'What authority?' snorted Mrs. Green. 'Who do you
think you are? Those kids have got the right idea—a
good kick is what you need, Joe!'

'Lavinia!' interrupted Patience. 'Please, can we stop

all this squabbling? Emmy, take Mr Ormond to see your puppy, but supper won't be long, so make sure you bring him back to the kitchen in time to wash his hands.'

Emmy looked up at James confidingly. 'She's very bossy.'

'Yes, I noticed that,' said James, not particularly interested in this puppy but fatalistically accepting that he was going to see it whether he wanted to or not. These children took after their sister. They were steamrollers in human form. Just like her.

CHAPTER THREE

WHEN he had seen and admired the children's puppy, all big eyes and muddy paws, rescued from the garden shed where the old man had locked it and where it was whining piteously, James was given a tour by Emmy, who appeared to have made him her property and was determined that he should see everything she considered of interest in the garden. The puppy skidded along with them, tail wagging excitedly.

James gazed obediently at the golden trumpets of the daffodils, bluetits nesting in a home-made nestbox nailed onto the side of a fir tree, a sea of green shoots which would soon, Emmy assured him, become a sea of bluebells, and the cedar tree into which young Toby climbed to stare down at the rest of them, his skinny legs in grubby jeans dangling over a branch while the puppy scampered through the long wild grass, barking in all the secret places between shrubs which Emmy said were the dens.

'We have one each. This is mine,' she proudly informed him, squeezing through thick branches into the small space behind and peering out at him. 'I don't let anyone else in—but you can come in, Man.'

'I can't, I'm too big,' James said, wishing he had had a den like that when he was small. The gardeners who had looked after his father's garden would never have stood for him having a den in their immaculately maintained grounds, however. He'd only been allowed in the garden when somebody was with him, in case he did some damage.

'Don't be sad, Man,' Emmy said, emerging again and taking his hand, giving it a comforting pat. 'Never mind. Thomas will let you play in his den, won't you, Thomas?'

By then James had identified the two Kirby boys; Thomas must be ten and Toby fourteen. He had not liked to ask about their parents; somehow he sensed that both were dead—they were certainly never mentioned. It was Patience the children talked about.

'Sure, okay,' Thomas said, pushing aside some leaves to display his own den, which contained an old log on which were arranged a litter of leaves. 'See? I've got a table.' He thought. 'And it can be a chair, too, if you want it.'

With the children gazing at him expectantly James felt he had to bend and squeeze himself through the shrubs into the small space.

'You can sit down on the chair,' Thomas kindly offered, joining him.

James sat, with difficulty, because his legs were too long, and Thomas let the branches swing back. At once they were plunged into green shadow made by the last of the light flickering down through the leaves. They could only dimly see the others, outside.

'Great, isn't it?' Thomas prompted.

'Magic,' James said, wishing his vocabulary with children was not so limited. He had had almost no experience with them since his own childhood. It must be very sad for Emmy, Thomas and Toby to have no parents; they were lucky that they had an older sister. His mouth twisted—come on, be honest! he told himself. These kids have a happier life than you ever did, don't they?

His father had never been unkind to him, but he'd rarely been around anyway. Given the choice, James would have swapped places with the Kirby children any day; he could see that their lives were busy, cheerful and full of affection, thanks to their sister.

'How old is Patience?' he asked Thomas.

'Twenty-three next week. How old are you?'

James grimaced. 'A lot older than that.'

'Do you have any children?'

'No.' He had never wanted any; suddenly he wondered if his life would have been richer, warmer, if he had had some.

'Are you married?' Thomas had the curt curiosity of a detective; his questions came like bullets.

'No.'

'Got a girlfriend?'

Warily James said, 'Maybe. Have you?'

Thomas laughed. 'Maybe.'

James liked him. They both jumped as, from somewhere in the house, a loud voice yelled.

'Come in for supper, all of you, and bring Mr Ormond unless you've lost him.'

'Patience!' explained Thomas.

'I recognised her voice.' Not to mention the way she referred to him as if he were a parcel rather than a man. So she was almost twenty-three? He would have said she was younger; he had been sure she was closer to childhood than that. She had such soft, clear, glowing skin and such a direct gaze, none of the pretences or defences of adulthood. None of the manners, either, he thought grimly, remembering the way she had badgered and bamboozled him into coming here.

'There's a big gap between Patience and Toby, isn't

there?' Why had their parents waited so long to have another child?

'Our mum wasn't her mum!' Thomas told him pityingly, as if he ought to have known, or at least guessed that. 'Patience's mum died when she was born and our Dad married our Mum and had us.'

James stared. 'Oh, then she isn't...?'

Before he could finish that sentence Thomas gruffly and with obvious indignation said, 'But she's our sister, all the same! She was five when Dad married our mum, and she loved our mum; she told us lots of times. She loved having a mum like everybody else, and then when we were born that made us a real family, Patience says.'

James had never felt so clumsy and insensitive in his life. 'Of course,' he quickly said, going dark red.

The leaves parted and Emmy peered in. 'We'd better go in; she can get very cross if you're late for meals.'

James was relieved to escape from the boy's clear, accusing stare, and began crawling out through the bushes. So, she was their half-sister? They obviously adored her, and she understood them—well, she was barely out of childhood herself. Twenty-three. That wasn't very old. He remembered being that young. With difficulty. Well, he was not staying for supper; he would ring for a taxi at once and get back to the safety and peace of his own home.

Somehow, though, the prospect did not appeal— Barny and Enid would be out. He would have to rummage around for a snack for himself, probably ending up with a cheese sandwich or something equally easy to prepare, then spend the rest of the evening alone in an empty house.

Of course, he could go to his club or a restaurant, but that wasn't an exciting prospect, either. Had his life always been this lonely and empty? Or was he just depressed for some inexplicable reason?

The young Kirbys led him back down the winding paths of the garden to the house; their friends disappeared in all directions to their own homes and James followed Emmy through a door into what turned out to be the kitchen.

It was enormous: high-ceilinged, painted yellow, with green cupboards—a cosy, comfortable room, full of a delicious smell of food. A great pan was boiling away on an old range, filling the air with steam, and beside it was another pan which bubbled and gave off that marvellous smell of vegetables and herbs. At the well-scrubbed deal table stood a woman grating mounds of cheese without looking up.

'Wash your hands and be quick; this is nearly ready!' dictated Patience, taking hold of the handle of the pan and pouring the contents into a sink. James went over to watch her, and discovered pasta filling a huge colander with golden, steaming coils. His stomach clenched in sudden hunger; he loved spaghetti. He looked into the pot still cooking: tomato, mushrooms, red, green and yellow peppers, and a strong odour of basil, chives, onions and garlic. His nose had already identified most of them.

'Have you washed your hands?' Patience demanded, looking round at him sternly, as if he was one of the children.

James opened and shut his mouth like a goldfish, meaning to tell her that he was not eating but so hungry he knew he would not give the words any credibility.

'Come on, Man,' Emmy told him, dragging him away. 'She gets cross if you aren't sitting down at the table when she brings the supper in!'

They washed in a small room next to the kitchen, then Emmy pulled him down a chilly corridor into a big room full of people, all sitting around an enormous table. James was horrorstruck by meeting so many strangers all at once; in self-defence he bowed slightly, saying in a pompous voice, 'Good evening, how do you do? I'm James Ormond.'

There was a general murmur in reply. 'Hallo,' some said. Others said, 'Good evening.' James looked hurriedly from face to face—was one of them his mother? But he did not recognise any of the old ladies who bobbed their heads and smiled. Lavinia was not one of them; he remembered her. She must have been the woman he had glimpsed in the kitchen, helping Patience.

Emmy pulled him down onto a chair next to her just as Patience came into the room wheeling a trolley on which sat large green soup plates of pasta, which was now well mixed with the sauce he had seen cooking. Toby and some of the old ladies helped her put the plates in front of each person around the table.

Patience stood behind her own chair. 'Whose turn is it to say grace? Emmy?'

'Yes, me. Lord, thank you for our daily bread,' Emmy said at a gallop.

Everyone else said, 'Amen.'

'Help yourself to cheese and bread,' Patience told James briskly, putting a plate before him. The smell of the spaghetti was heavenly.

He took a chunk of granary bread from the big wicker basket in the middle of the table, sprinkled some grated cheese over his pasta and picked up his fork and spoon. He often ate Italian food and deftly wound spirals of pasta onto his fork and lifted it to his mouth while Emmy watched him admiringly.

'How d'you do that? Mine falls off all the time.'

Everyone looked at James, who flushed under their eyes. 'Like this,' he said, showing Emmy how to separate some spaghetti, then twist her fork round and round. 'Now you try.'

She slowly copied him, the tip of her pink tongue between her lips. Pink with success, she lifted the fork towards her mouth and the spaghetti flopped off again. Everyone laughed.

'It's slippery stuff,' James quickly said as Emmy reddened, her mouth quivering. Like most small children, she was very sensitive to mockery; James couldn't bear to see her look like that.

'Like pink worms,' Thomas added. 'Carcful they don't wriggle off your plate, Em, and go down under your clothes.' He held up a long, drooping strand of spaghetti and waved it at his sister, who shrieked.

'Stop that, Tom.' Patience leaned over and cut some of the little girl's spaghetti into short lengths. 'Use your spoon if you like, Em.'

Emmy began to eat much faster, and for a few moments there was silence as people ate with bent heads.

James loved every mouthful; even Enid did not make pasta better than this. Simple food needed to be perfectly cooked to work, and this was perfectly cooked pasta. Patience was a very good cook.

'Wine?' asked Patience, offering James a large china jug.

'Oh…er, thank you.' He looked a little suspiciously at the contents; it would be cheap stuff and no doubt more like vinegar than wine, but it was either that or the jugs of water or milk which the children were drinking.

Patience poured wine into his glass; James very warily tried a mouthful, rolling it round his tongue before he risked swallowing. Well, it was rough but it wasn't sour; it had a country taste which matched the vegetables in the sauce. He took another mouthful; yes, it was really quite pleasant. He had once spent a month touring the Italian countryside, and this was the sort of table wine you were served in a remote Italian village in the summer. He had happy memories of sitting under a vine at some trattoria with a glass of this rough local wine and a plate of pasta served with a sauce of either tomato or pesto.

He finished his meal with a sigh of completion. The empty plate was suddenly whisked away; the table was being cleared. Was the meal over? He looked sideways at Patience, who appeared to be able to read minds.

'There's plums and custard now,' she said. 'Our own plums; I bottled them myself last autumn. They aren't very big but they've got a nice flavour. We grow as much stuff as we can, especially vegetables.'

'Yes, I saw the vegetable garden on my tour of the garden.' James looked around; nobody was listening to them—they were all too busy talking to each other. Offhandedly he asked, 'So, when am I going to meet...? Where is...?'

'Where's your mother?' Yes, she could definitely read minds. He nodded, hoping she would keep her own voice down.

He didn't want the whole table to know what they were talking about, although no doubt they were aware why he was here—even the children, who seemed to know everything that was going on in this house.

'She's upstairs,' Patience said softly, 'in bed; she wasn't too well today. She does come downstairs, for a few hours, on her better days. I encourage her to do that because it's so depressing to be stuck upstairs alone all the time; I think she needs company. She certainly always looks happier afterwards. But she wasn't up to it today; she knew I was going to try to see you and it upset her, made her very nervous, so I told her to stay in bed. I'll take you up to see her after supper.'

He did not want to see his mother. He stared at nothing, feeling anger burning in his chest, suddenly afraid he might make a fool of himself, might lose control, lose his temper or, even worse, cry. He had learnt at a very young age not to show his feelings, not to let anyone guess what was going on inside him. The idea of breaking down in public was a nightmare. He couldn't risk it, especially in front of this girl's clear, direct gaze. She might be sorry for him. A shiver ran down his spine at the very idea. That was the very last thing he would want.

Several of the older women were clearing the table, going out to the kitchen with the used plates and returning with a huge bowl of red plums in a glistening syrup. Full of sugar, thought James glumly; full of calories, too. As for the calories in those jugs of yellow custard; he would hate to think what they added up to! When he ate fruit it was fresh and low in calories. He would not have either plums or custard!

The children went round the table skimming small bowls into place in front of everyone. He opened his mouth to tell them not to give him one but too late; Thomas had already hurried on. A moment later the bowl of plums appeared in front of him. 'Help yourself,' Patience invited.

'Thanks, but I really don't think I...'

'Try them, they're delicious.'

He couldn't face an argument—his nerves were already jumping like ants under his skin; politely he took several plums, adding a trickle of yellow custard. That also looked over-sweet and sickly.

Emmy leaned her head towards him, whispering, 'Sometimes we have ice-cream but it isn't an ice-cream day.'

'That's a pity. I like ice-cream.'

'So do I,' she sighed.

James felt something inside him stir, a warmth he had never felt before, a tenderness, a sense of kinship, as if she were his own child. It was absurd. He would probably never set eyes on her again. That idea made him frown. He had only known her for a couple of hours yet he stupidly felt he would miss her if he never saw her again. He watched her pushing her spoon around in the bowl without taking anything. 'Do you like plums?' he whispered.

She made a face, darting a secret glance at Patience, who was talking across the table to Toby, unaware of them.

'They're better than prunes.'

'Not much,' said James, wrinkling his nose.

Emmy giggled. 'No, they aren't, are they? Patience doesn't like it if we don't try everything, though.' She watched James eat his last plum. 'You can have one of mine, if you like,' she generously offered, hurriedly pushing it into his bowl while Patience's attention was elsewhere.

James ate it without a word; he would have eaten it even if it had been utterly loathsome just to get Emmy's grateful smile. Across the table Thomas and Toby winked at him. He winked back and felt Patience turn to stare at them all with suspicion.

'What have you been up to?'

James turned, lifting a cold, haughty eyebrow. 'I beg your pardon?'

'Hmm,' she said, getting up. 'You don't fool me.' But she didn't pursue the matter. 'Come on, we'll take coffee upstairs. Boys, homework. Emmy, have you learnt your spellings?'

Emmy nodded.

'Toby, make her spell all of them for you. After that, half an hour's television, then get washed and into bed. I'll check on you later.'

James followed her out of the room into the kitchen, where one of the women was already busy making coffee. She turned to smile at them.

'Hallo, enjoy your supper?' This time he recognised her white hair and bright blue eyes.

'Yes, thank you, Lavinia.'

Patience gave him a surprised look as she set about laying a tray with cups and saucers, spoons, a sugar bowl of brown sugar lumps and a small jug of cream, ending with a pot of coffee.

'I'll take that,' James politely said, picking it up.

'Thank you. It is pretty heavy.' Patience walked out of the kitchen and turned up the wide polished oak stairs and onto a landing from which several corridors branched off. Rows of doors, all closed, confronted him, and at the end of one corridor a narrow flight of stairs going up to another floor. How many rooms were there? he wondered. This rambling old house must be larger than it looked from the outside.

'How many guests do you have?'

'At the moment, four men and three women. If we had any more than that they would have to share a room, which I don't like—privacy is so important to people at any age, but especially someone who has no home of their own any more. They don't have much else. No family—or often any friends.'

James shivered, as if a ghost had walked over his grave. He knew what it was like to have nothing and no one. After his mother had gone he had felt abandoned, forsaken—lonely and cold in that luxurious, empty house, with his father never there, no brothers and sisters, no friends, only servants for company. It had been bad enough for a child, how did it feel when you were old? Did the irony ever occur to his mother? His father had always told him that whatever you did always came back on your own head—good or evil, you were always repaid in kind.

Patience was still talking, but she was watching him and he was beginning to be afraid that she could always read his thoughts, so he pushed away his own memories and concentrated on what she was saying.

'Our rooms are all furnished and they can't bring anything with them except a few little things—photographs, books, the odd ornament. Some of them have a radio or TV of their own, and I allow that so long as they keep the volume down and don't disturb anyone else. It makes them feel more at home to have some of their own stuff around them.'

James stood, holding the tray in front of him like a butler, staring down at her. 'What on earth makes you do it?' he broke out harshly. 'Why fill your home with strangers, do all this work...? Surely it would be much easier to sell this house and buy somewhere smaller and get a job. You wouldn't have to work so hard; you would have set hours and more fun.'

'This is the children's home; they don't want to live anywhere else. I promised them when our parents died that I would keep the house and we would all stay together—nothing would be different. I couldn't go out to work then because Emmy was too young, and running a guest-house seemed the perfect answer.'

He wished he hadn't shouted at her but it was too late to regret losing his temper—and why had he suddenly felt so angry that his head nearly blew off just because some total stranger was doing something he felt was crazy and inexplicable? Why should he care if she chose to work like a slave, taking care of all these people?

'What happened to your parents?' he muttered.

'They were killed in a car crash three years ago. A lorry driver had a heart attack at the wheel and smashed right into their car head-on. At least they didn't suffer. They died on impact, apparently.'

'Three years ago?' James thought aloud. 'How old was Emmy?' Now why did he want to know that? He seemed to be losing all control of his mind, thinking and saying things that would never have occurred to him before today.

'Three years old, poor baby.'

James winced. 'It must have hit her hard.'

Patience sighed, nodding. 'She regressed—turned back into a baby. She didn't talk or walk, burst into tears over nothing, had nightmares at night, called for her mother—shock takes a long time to wear off; it's like a bruise but on the inside instead of the outside. I couldn't have left her with strangers; she needed to be with someone who loved her. I had to be here for her all the time. And the boys were difficult to deal with, too; it took them another way. Toby started stealing from local shops, swearing, bullying other boys at school, and Thomas wet the bed, wouldn't eat, wouldn't do what you told him, couldn't concentrate on his schoolwork.'

Grimly, James said, 'Boys are taught not to show their

feelings, so they have to find another way of dealing with the pain.' He had never expressed it at all; he had internalised it, wrapped it up and put it away out of sight at the back of his mind where he suddenly realised it had lain all this time, festering and every so often beginning to leak out without him understanding why he got those jabs of anger and distress from nowhere.

Looking up at him, Patience smiled gently. 'It is terrifying, having parents vanish like that, out of the blue.'

They were both talking about him as much as her brothers and sister. He looked away, his face pale.

'It made the children so insecure they no longer felt they could trust anyone not to disappear; they were afraid I might go next. So you see why I couldn't have sold this house.'

Yes, he could see the predicament she had been in, but he could not believe she should have opened the house as a hotel. 'How do they feel about having all these old people around all the time, though? I shouldn't think they would want other people sharing your attention, not to mention taking up so much of your energy.' He knew he wouldn't like it.

'Oh, but they love it—they don't have grandparents, and I think children need contact with the older generation; there's a natural sympathy between children and old people. They're far closer in spirit than parents are with children; parents have too many responsibilities, too much to do running a home, finding money, doing practical things. They're the ones who discipline and feel they have to keep nagging at the children to do better. Old people have left all that behind and are sitting back, enjoying life, the way children do.

'For instance, Joe has taught the boys gardening, although he gets cross now and then, and Emmy helps

Lavinia in the kitchen; she likes being in there, measuring flour, beating eggs, spooning out jam—Lavinia is teaching her how to cook, which is fun for both of them. Lavinia has no grandchildren, you see, and she should have had them; she makes a lovely grandma.'

'Was it Lavinia who cooked the supper? I thought it was you.'

'We did it together; Lavinia was a professional cook at one time, I've learnt a lot from her.' Patience looked at the tray he still held. 'That coffee must be getting cold and we ought to go in and see your mother. She's probably wondering what is going on out here! She must be able to hear us talking.'

James was frozen to the spot; he felt as if his feet had grown down into the carpet and he couldn't move. Patience stared up at him, her bright hazel eyes probing his face. She was at it again—reading minds!

'Come on!'

'Stop pushing me around, Miss Kirby!' He used his most cutting, incisive voice. 'I'll go in there when I'm ready.'

'Don't be scared,' she said in a gentle voice, at which he reddened angrily.

'I'm nothing of the kind! What are you talking about? Scared!'

She smiled at him, then walked away down the corridor, and James slowly, reluctantly followed. Patience stopped at a door, turned the handle and opened it on a scene of lamplit cosiness.

His eyes leapt around the room nervously, taking in the fact that it was a square bedroom which was also a sitting room, containing a red-velvet-covered chaise-longue of Edwardian style, ornate and sensual, heaped with velvet cushions in several colours, on which reposed a trio of battered old teddy bears. Beside it was a small, round table on which stood a brass pot of pink and white hyacinths in bloom, their scent rich and sweet, and in the far corner a bed covered by a patchwork duvet. A woman lay in the bed, leaning against a pile of pillows, her face turned towards the door.

James couldn't refuse to move—he would have looked ridiculous, and he hated above everything to look ridiculous—so, walking like a robot, he crossed the room and put the tray down on the table, taking only one brief, hurried glance before looking away again.

'Hallo, James,' his mother said, and incredibly he knew that voice immediately; the timbre of it had deepened, grown husky, but he found he had never forgotten it.

He had to look at her then. Her hair, like Lavinia's, was white, but had a faint pink rinse in it; James stared, thinking of candy floss at a fair. It had that wispy texture, like thistledown, unreal and insubstantial. He had been remembering her hair as dark, like his own, sleek and long and silky.

She held out her hand as if he were a stranger come to visit her, and of course they were just that—strangers.

His feet felt like lead but with an effort he somehow moved them and took her hand; once his had been swallowed up in hers but now it was the other way around. Her fingers were tiny and cold. His hand could have crushed them.

He did not know what to say. What did you say to someone you had not seen for so many years? Someone you had been very angry with for so long?

But was that fragile creature in the bed the woman he had hated all this time? The last time he'd seen her she had been young, beautiful, smelling of French perfume and full of gaiety. There was no resemblance between the two images; only her voice remained to haunt him, like the voice of a ghost whispering down the chill passages of memory.

'Hallo,' he said, hating this situation and hating Patience for getting him into it. It was all her fault—who did she think she was? What gave her the right to prod and push people into doing things they did not want to do?

'Sit down,' Patience said, as if he was one of those children downstairs whose lives she managed so certainly and self-confidently. She pushed a chair forward for him; the seat of it banged into the back of his knees and forced him to sink down onto it. 'Let's have the coffee, shall we, before it gets cold?'

Sitting down gave him something to do. He crossed his legs, smoothing down his trousers, and suddenly noticed specks of mud on them—he must have got that when he'd crawled into and out of Thomas's den. Crossly, he brushed at the specks, but they had dried hard. The trousers would need to go to the cleaners tomorrow. Accepting the coffee Patience handed him gave him something else to do; he slowly stirred the spoon round and round, staring down into the cup.

'Sugar?'

'No, thank you.' James turned his smouldering eyes towards her, hoping she could read his mind this time—he was thinking about what he wanted to say to her, the blistering words he would use if they were alone.

She grinned at him, her hazel eyes dancing. Oh, yes, she had read his mind and it merely amused her. She was one of the strangest women he had ever met, at one and the same time too young and too old for him. Too young in years and experience of the world; too bossy to live with.

What am I thinking about? he asked himself in horror. Live with? Flushed and furious, with himself as well as her, he looked away, stirring his coffee.

'Would you like me to go away for a while, leave you two alone?' Patience asked.

Both James and his mother said, *'No!'* together, in a rush.

So his mother wasn't easy with the idea of talking to him, either? he realised, looking at her and seeing now how thin and pale she was. You could see all the bones in her face, all the fine blue veins under her skin. She was as insubstantial as a cobweb, and yet he could see a sort of beauty in her still; time had worn away the mask and laid bare the striking bone structure of that face.

'Patience says you lived abroad for a long time, in Europe,' he said politely, making small-talk with this stranger.

'France, Spain, Italy,' she nodded. 'I travelled quite a bit.'

'Singing, Patience says?'

She smiled. 'That's right—do you remember, I used to sing to you when you were a baby? Only when your father was out, of course; he hated me to sing, although I was singing when he met me—that's how we met, I was singing with a small band, at a London hotel. Your father had dinner there, with friends, and he came back again, alone, the following night and asked me out. I think that was the first impulse move he had ever made. He wasn't an impulsive man as a rule, but he was younger, then; his real nature hadn't begun to show.'

'I won't listen to you running my father down!' James began to get up and she threw out a hand pleadingly.

'I didn't mean to upset you! I'm sorry. Don't go, James.'

He was aware of Patience hovering, her face concerned, and slowly sat down again.

His mother sighed and relaxed again, her frail hand lying on the duvet, fingers almost skeletal, ringless. She had always worn rings, he remembered: her gold wedding band, her ruby and diamond engagement ring, a big diamond his father had given her the day after James had been born. Her fingers had glittered when she moved her hands.

'I didn't know you had ever been a singer; nobody ever told me that.' What else had he never been told? Yet, oddly, he did remember her singing, with him sitting on her knee, at the piano in the drawing room; she had played nursery rhymes for him, sung old folk songs. How strange—he had forgotten that entirely until now. Memory played strange tricks.

She smiled wryly. 'I'm not surprised—your father didn't want anyone to know. He regretted marrying me while we were on honeymoon, I think. His family didn't approve, his friends were standoffish, and, really, we had nothing in common, either. It was a mistake, on both sides; I was a bit dazzled by him for a while. He had class—good-looking, nice clothes, lots of money. I felt like Cinderella when she met the Prince, and it was a convenient escape route from all my problems.'

Coldly, James said, 'So you didn't actually ever love him?'

'I thought I did, for a while. I told you, I was dazzled, but I want to be honest and tell you the whole truth. The band and I weren't doing too well—this was the late fifties, of course. In America there was Elvis, and a lot of rock films were being made there. Here, the Beatles were just around the corner, and a host of other rock bands. Kids didn't go for our sort of music; we were all in our twenties and we were already going out of fashion.

'We had a struggle getting work, even more of a problem finding the money to pay rent and eat. I had no rich family to back me; my father had died and my mother was living with a guy I didn't like. When your father asked me to marry him I jumped at it. I really did think I was in love, James. In a way, I was for a while—in love with a dream. It was only after we were married that real life broke up our illusions and the terrible gaps began to show.'

'You mean you met another man.' James was trying not to lose control again, but his anger burnt in his voice.

'I'm being honest, James! Yes, I did meet someone else, but that came later. First, I realised my marriage didn't work. Your father wished he had never married me; he had never really loved me at all.'

'He never married again!' He couldn't help his voice rising, thick and bitter. Patience jumped and his mother shrank back in the bed.

But she still answered him in a threadlike voice. 'He should never have married in the first place. James, he was a cold, indifferent man; he didn't need a wife. He had a secretary and servants, and his relationship with them was on a footing he understood. He paid them and kept them at a distance. You can't do that with a wife.'

Or with a child, he thought with a pang. That exactly described his relationship with his father. The coldness and emptiness of his childhood made sense of what his mother was telling him. He had told himself that it was her fault that his father was chilly and remote, but maybe she was telling the truth and his father had always been that way? Yet she had left him with that man and gone away for ever!

He looked at her with bitterness. 'Then why did you leave me behind, with him?'

But he had had enough. He didn't wait for her to give him some soothing answer—what could she say? She could only lie. She had gone away and left him in a frozen wasteland, and James wasn't listening to any more.

Giving Patience a resentful look, because it was she who had inflicted all this on him, he got up and walked out, went down the stairs and out of the front door, slamming it behind him.

He was never going back there again.

CHAPTER FOUR

JAMES was striding out of the gate when he realised that he had no transport. Damn! He should have rung a taxi. Where on earth was he, anyway? He had no idea apart from the fact that it was in North London. He had been too absorbed in that maddening little redhead to take any notice of the route Barny had taken—he tried to remember any landmark they'd passed but couldn't even recall the name of the road. The house was called The Cedars, that much he was sure about, but that was it, and now that it was dark he was totally lost.

Now what did he do? He wasn't going back into the house; that would make him look silly after that melodramatic exit. When you have slammed a door you don't open it again and say, Oh, excuse me, could you call me a taxi?

This was a very quiet road, but it was not a long one—he could see traffic moving at the far end: headlights of cars, a lorry trundling along, then what he believed to be a one-decker red bus. It must be a main road, and there must be a public phone-box or maybe a public house somewhere around. He was still in London, of course—around him stretched streets in all directions, and the night sky was lit with that strange yellow glare which London skies have at night, all the street lights and house lights blazing upwards, so bright that you can rarely see a star or even the moon.

James was about to begin walking when someone ran towards him out of the night, a thin, dark shape which

69

had an unearthly glow around its feet and made him apprehensive until it passed under a street lamp and was revealed as a skinny blond boy in trainers with glowing soles, jeans and a ribbed black sweater that clung to his chest. James stood still and aimed a smile at him as he drew level. 'Hallo, can you tell me where I am?'

He received in reply a look of pitying disdain. 'You don't know where you are? Well, at least you admit it. My parents don't know where they are; they think it's still the nineteen-sixties, and they won't admit time didn't stop when they were on the hippy trail.'

James forced himself to stay patient. Was everyone he met today going to be crazy? 'How sad for you, but it could have been worse. They could have thought Queen Victoria was still alive—hippy parents must be quite sympathetic by comparison. Tell me, is there a telephone box anywhere around here?'

'I don't think so—why?'

'Oddly enough because I want to make a telephone call.'

'Oh, very witty. You should get a mobile. Wake up, man, and smell the coffee. It's later than you think. Any minute we'll be in the twenty-first century—do you realise that?'

Irritating little prat, thought James. He thinks he is so funny. 'Yes, I do actually. It has been in my thoughts constantly for some years.'

'Yeah, right,' the boy said with disbelief, but grinned, taking James's remark for humour when it was the simple truth.

Anyone involved in business had to be aware of the coming millenium and all that it would mean, especially for Europeans—not so much because of a change of century as because during the next decade many things would be changing for the peoples of Europe. But James wanted to get home, so he asked the boy, 'What is the name of this part of London?'

'Get real, man. If you got here, you must know where you are.'

'Someone drove me here.'

'Oh. Right. This is Muswell Hill.'

A sigh escaped James. Of course. How on earth had he forgotten that? 'And the name of the road?'

The boy opened his mouth, but instead of answering gave a strangled groan. 'Patience.'

James started. Violently. 'What did you say?' Were his ears playing tricks on him, or, even worse, his brain? Had this boy really said her name, or was he becoming so obsessed that whatever anyone said to him entered his brain in that one word? Patience.

The boy wasn't listening, wasn't looking at him. He was taking slow steps towards the gate James had just come through, staring fixedly, and he was babbling.

'I have to talk to you—I just had a big row with them—they have no right to run my life. I'm not a child; I told them so. They said I was too young to know what I was doing, and so were you, so I just walked out on them. I got so angry. I won't be treated like that.'

James stared at the gate. He wasn't imagining anything. She stood there, leaning on the gate, the light on her hair turning it silvery, as if someone had sifted sugar all over the bright red strands, making her look as delicate and insubstantial as a dream, and this boy was gazing at her as if that was exactly what she was—a dream.

Patience looked past the boy at James. 'You need a taxi. I've rung for one for you.'

The boy's head swung; he glowered at James, looking even sulkier. 'Do you know this guy?' Apparently he resented the fact. 'He's out of his tree—he asked me where he was. Has he got amnesia, or is he just plain nuts?'

Patience opened the gate. 'Don't be rude, Col. You'd better come in but you can't stay long. I don't want your father roaring round here shouting at me. He was very rude last time.'

'He thinks you're after my money.'

'His money, he means. You haven't got any. And if you don't pass your exams you never will have any; you won't be able to get a job when you leave college.' Patience let him into the drive and gave James a cool glance. 'The taxi shouldn't be long. You won't forget that your mother will be sixty next Wednesday, will you?'

Unrevealingly, James asked her, 'When's your birthday?'

'Same day.'

He blinked at that. 'You're not serious. The same day?'

'Who is he?' the boy demanded, running a hostile inspection over him. 'Dresses like someone's father. Some sort of businessman? What's he doing here? Has he dumped his poor old mother on you?'

Rage burned inside James; he hadn't felt so aggressive for years, but something about this kid made him feel quite homicidal. 'Do you want a punch on the nose?' he snarled.

'Huh! Try it and see what you'll get!' The boy came back towards him, skinny and very young and trying to look much older and tougher, his chin up and his face dark red with temper.

Patience moved into his path, barring his way. 'Go

into the house, Colin! You were rude to Mr Ormond; you deserve a punch on the nose.'

'Ormond?' Colin stared at him, bristling. 'That guy? I didn't recognise him; the photos of him in newspapers make him look much younger and better looking. I suppose they touch them up.'

That didn't improve James's temper, especially when he caught Patience trying not to smile, her wide, generous mouth quivering, her hazel eyes dancing.

She gave Colin a little push. 'Go in, before you go too far.'

He already had. Teeth clenched, James pushed his hands into his trouser pockets, his shoulders squared and his body tense as a bowstring.

'Aren't you coming?' the boy asked Patience.

'I won't be long. I just want a word with Mr Ormond about his mother.'

'Tell him to take care of her himself!' The boy turned away, along the drive, towards the house, the shrubs and trees moving and whispering in the wind, his dark shadow floating silently on the path.

Looking down at her heart-shaped face, the wild mop of red curls, the full, soft mouth, James asked between his teeth, 'Is he your boyfriend?'

She gave him a wide-eyed, reproving stare. 'None of your business.'

True—not that that made him calmer. On the contrary. Feeling as if his head might blow off in pure rage, James almost yelled, 'Coming from you, that's rich. You've been interfering in my life, asking personal questions, passing judgements on me, ordering me around all day!'

'Shh!' She turned to shoot a look up the drive. 'Colin might hear you and decide you are bullying me. Then he'd come rushing back and hit you. He's in a very belligerent mood at the moment.'

'You really think I would stand still and let him hit me without hitting him first?' Did she think he was scared of that boy?

'That's what I'm afraid of,' she confessed. 'I don't want you hurting him.'

'How sweet and protective,' James sneered. What on earth did she see in the boy? He scowled, admitting the truth to himself—well, it was obvious, wasn't it? The boy was her own age group, of course. They would have their whole world in common, all the things a generation shares—the same taste in music, books, films, the same jokes, same gossip, same political attitudes, same hopes for the future.

A car engine sounded at the far end of the road. 'Here's your taxi,' Patience said. She put a hand on his wrist; James stiffened, looking down at it, intensely aware of those small, warm, soft fingers moving on his skin.

'Please come and see your mother again. I know it isn't easy for you to forget that she went away and left you, but everyone makes mistakes. Try to forgive her. Give her a chance, get to know her again—don't just turn your back and walk away.'

James wasn't really listening; he was the prey of disturbing impulses he had never felt before. Unable to take his eyes off her face, he had to fight to stop himself kissing her; her lips were so full and generous, sensually promising, pink as summer roses, he ached to taste them, to smell that soft, smooth skin, get close enough to see the gold glints in those big, hazel eyes and those funny, sandy little lashes...

What would it feel like? He would give anything to

find out. Even as a very young man he had never felt such a driving desire to kiss a girl, but he would not make a fool of himself. She would probably slap him or scream, and that boy would come rushing out here and start a fight. James was not scared of the boy, but he was terrified of the embarrassment of a scene out here in the road, terrified of looking ridiculous.

The taxi drew up behind them. Dragging his gaze from her face, James turned away, trying to be relieved to be escaping but in fact not wanting to go.

As he got into the taxi she called, 'Come to supper on my birthday—next Wednesday, remember. Bring your mother a present, not just flowers. Seven o'clock.'

James didn't commit himself to a yes or no; he sank back on the seat and told the driver his Regent's Park address. The taxi drove off. James looked at the gate, but she had vanished. He felt for a second that he had imagined her, she had never been here at all.

But she was only too real. This morning he hadn't known her name, or even that she existed; now his head was crammed with a dozen images of her and he felt as if he had always known her, all his life. Staring back at her house, he saw moonlight playing among the bare branches of trees, turning the rivers of daffodils silver. Most of the windows were now brightly lit; the children and old people would be going to bed, the house growing quiet downstairs; only Patience and that boy would still be up soon.

What exactly was going on between them? Did they kiss? Make love? The boy couldn't be more than twenty; Patience was three years older. At that age, that made her an 'older woman'—was that why the boy's parents didn't approve? What did they think went on between their precious son and this *femme fatale*?

He couldn't imagine them in bed together. His teeth ground together. He didn't want to imagine it.

As the taxi turned into a busy main road and headed south towards Regent's Park he scowled out of the window, his long, lean body sunk into the seat, swaying as the taxi turned corners sharply, his hands in his jacket pockets, his features set in a smouldering glare. It was none of his business what they did. Why should it matter to him?

But it did, however hard he tried to pretend otherwise.

On Saturday evening he had dinner with Fiona. Everyone in the restaurant stared at her—the men with admiration and desire, because she was dazzlingly beautiful, the women with dislike, because their men couldn't take their eyes off her, and with envy, because they wished they looked like her.

Her taste was impeccable. Tonight she was wearing a daring outfit by one of her favourite designers; James vaguely recognised the style—a mixture of elegance and high drama: a dark green skirt clinging close to her slender hips and a white satin bodice with a deep V-neckline, the back of the dress rearing up into a pleated, gold-tipped collar which framed the back of her head.

'Do you like it?' she asked him.

'You look like an arum lily. Isn't it a little uncomfortable, though?'

'It's only for special occasions.' She studied the menu and James studied her.

'Is this a special occasion?'

'Isn't it always when we see each other?' Her voice was as cool as a refrigerator, her eyes like the North Pole, although she smiled and her words had a flirtatious ring.

I've said something to annoy her, thought James—what? He never quite knew what women were thinking even when he heard what they were saying. There was some indefinable communication gap, as though they came from another culture and had had to learn to speak the same language as men without ever quite catching on to the nuances.

'I think I'll start with this melon surprise—I wonder what the surprise is?' Fiona said, and the waiter enlightened her.

'Balls of melon, madam, with melon sorbet and peach sorbet, assorted green leaves and sliced strawberries.'

'I'll have that—and then I'll have sole with a green salad.'

The food was typical of the meals they always ate together. Fiona was constantly dieting, careful always to eat low-calorie, low-fat food. James thought of the pasta with the very high-calorie sauce, the heaped grated cheese, the bread, the rough, red peasant wine he had had at supper two nights ago. That would have made Fiona shudder; she wouldn't have touched any of it with a barge pole. She liked her food exquisite, delicate, classy—like herself.

If you measured women in food, what did that make Patience Kirby? A little smile pulled at his mouth as he stared at the menu but saw instead her heart-shaped face, her big eyes, that wide, generous, enchanting mouth.

'James?' Fiona prompted, impatient at his long silence.

'Same for me,' James said, and ordered a bottle of white wine. When the waiter had departed he asked Fiona, 'How is your father?' It was a safe question and saved him having to think. He quite liked her father, although the man was a little stuffy.

'He's off to the Far East for a series of meetings with major international players, so he has left me in charge. I'm going to be very busy until he gets back. His work-load added to mine makes for a twelve-hour day mini-mum, if I'm lucky.'

'What about the trip we were taking next weekend? Will you still be free for that?'

'To stay with Oliver and Peta? No, sorry, I can't make that. Dad won't be back until the week after.'

'In that case, I shan't go. It would be dull on my own. Olly is okay, but Peta is tedious. I'll plead pressure of work too.'

'We can't both drop out!'

'I'll simply tell them I won't come without you— they'll understand; they only ever invite couples.'

'That's true.'

'What's behind your father's trip, anyway?'

'He wants to find out more about the companies he is dealing with over there, and he can do that better on their turf, where he can actually see what they are doing rather than just swallow whatever information they choose to give us.'

'And it's a good excuse for a freebie?' he joked, but she did not smile, merely looked offended.

'Dad will be there to work, meet people, get new cli-ents—he doesn't joyride at the company's expense. Although if he wanted to he would be entitled—it is his company, after all.'

Yes, she is annoyed about something—but what? he thought, as the wine waiter arrived with their chilled wine. James tasted it, then said, 'Leave it in the ice bucket until our first course arrives, would you?'

He found out what was on Fiona's mind half an hour later, when they were eating their sole and had almost finished their bottle of wine. Fiona suddenly asked, 'Where were you on Thursday night?'

James stared blankly. 'Thursday night?'

'My father wanted to talk to you so he rang your home, but you weren't in—in fact, nobody was in. There was no reply. He kept ringing, right up till he went to bed at eleven.'

To his chagrin James felt himself going red, heat began to sting along his cheekbones. He looked down at his half-eaten fish, pretended to be concentrating on finding a non-existent bone among the meltingly smooth white fish.

Feigning a shrug, he said, 'I had dinner out, in town, because I'd given my staff a night off.'

'You didn't eat at the restaurant we'd booked—my father rang them and they said you had cancelled.'

'No, I—'

She interrupted his halting sentence. 'Or at your club, he tried there too.'

James looked up then, suddenly furious, the heat in his face now that of resentful irritation. 'What is this? Am I on trial for something? I suppose you'll tell me next that you've got a private detective following me around?'

She was as cool as ever, her eyes skimming his face, probably reading guilt in his flush. 'Don't be insulting! I was simply curious. I wondered where you had been that night, that's all!'

'I went to see someone I hadn't seen for years, as it happens.'

She waited, lifting one eyebrow, but James was not ready to talk about his mother, not yet. He filled his mouth with fish instead of saying anything else. Fiona laughed—the tinkling of ice in a champagne glass.

'An old flame?'

So that was what she had been imagining? She thought he had gone off for the night with some other woman!

How dared she put him through this in public? burned James, his teeth grinding together. She had no right. She wasn't his wife. Yet. He was beginning to wonder if she ever would be—was she really the sort of wife he wanted?

'No, an old woman,' he said curtly, and drank the last of his wine; it tasted bitter suddenly.

Her brows came together. 'Old woman? Who on earth...? Your old nanny?'

James had had enough. 'Isn't it obvious that I don't want to talk about it?' he bit out, pushing his plate away. 'Can we drop it?'

From then on it was a chilly evening, in every sense of the word. They were not totally silent—they were both too polite for that. They talked about business: about the City, about companies going broke, companies doing brilliantly, rumours of mergers, hints of monetary problems, whispers of take-overs. They did not linger over their coffee. They did not go dancing, as they frequently did on their dates. James drove Fiona home at once; they made occasional, cool remarks to each other, and when they reached her home she brushed a brief, cold kiss over his cheek before getting out of the car.

'Goodnight, James. Thank you for a lovely meal.'

'Goodnight, Fiona. Don't work too hard while your father is away.'

The conventional politeness was the only adult way of dealing with the gap which had just opened up between them. Or had it always been there? Had he ever really thought about Fiona?

It was time he did, and he would have the chance over the next week or two. It would give them both an excuse for a cooling off period, this trip of her father's. Driving home, James decided he ought to send her flowers tomorrow. Should the message say 'Sorry'? No. He wasn't lying; he wasn't sorry about anything he had said or done. Why should she put him through that inquisition? She didn't own him.

What should he say on the card? Just 'Love from'? Why not? It committed him to nothing. Everyone wrote something like that. Such a simple phrase...'love from'... It meant nothing.

A shiver ran down his spine. A week ago he had been almost sure he would marry her. Now... Well, did he want to spend the rest of his life under a searchlight like someone in a prison camp, behind barbed wire, with guards and dogs set to catch him if he tried to get out?

He knew he was being ridiculous, melodramatic—yet was he? What freedom would he have if Fiona had to know everything he did, everywhere he went, no doubt even what he thought?

It was time he took control of his own life and stopped drifting into deep waters. He had to make decisions about the future, think hard about how he wanted his life to be from now on.

He did not want to see his mother again, for a start. She had no right to walk back into his life after all these years and expect a warm welcome. They were total strangers now; she meant nothing to him. Patience Kirby had no business asking him to forget what his mother had done to him, how much she had hurt him, the loneliness and sadness of his childhood. He couldn't. She might be some sort of saint but he was not.

* * *

Sunday was cold and wet, the wind lashing across the green acres of Regent's Park and making the trees in his garden sway and moan. James didn't go out; he spent the entire day at home, mostly in his study, sitting in a green leather chair behind his large leather-topped desk studying complex financial graphs and the detailed accounts of a company who were new clients.

He had his usual Sunday breakfast: grapefruit, bacon and egg and toast and marmalade. His usual Sunday lunch: smoked salmon followed by roast beef and Yorkshire pudding with three vegetables, then a meltingly light lemon mousse and coffee. Barny and Enid were in the kitchen at the back; the rest of the house was empty and silent except for the deep tones of the grandfather clock in the hall. Normally he would have seen Fiona, or at least talked to her on the phone. Today nobody came, nobody rang. He might have lived on a desert island.

How many days in his life had passed like this? Routine, dry as dust, habit, cold as an iceberg—was that how his life had been, was going to be? He got up restlessly and walked to the window to look out at the wind-blown, dripping garden. Grey skies, wet slate roofs, emptiness—he felt the way he had when he was a boy, lonely and aching.

At six he went up to have his bath and stayed in the warm, scented water longer than usual; by the time he had dressed it was time for his pre-dinner ritual glass of sherry, except that tonight he drank whisky.

Barny came to tell him dinner was served and looked sharply at the glass of whisky he held, and then at the decanter whose dropped level gave away the fact that that was his second glass.

'Taking to drink? That won't help.'

'Mind your own business.' James walked out to eat what Enid had prepared for him and caught sight of his reflection in a mirror he passed: a tall, dark, frowning man, with cold eyes and a tight mouth. My God! I am beginning to look like my father, he thought, his chest contracting in a spasm of pain. That was the last thing he wanted. Maybe he should sell this damned house and go and live in the country, start growing roses, spend more time out of doors, sailing or playing golf? He did not want to end up a remote, chilly man who had never really been alive at all.

That was what she'd said. His mother. She had been honest about his father and he had resented it. But it was true and James did not want to end up that way.

By Monday the rain had slackened away to a light drizzle and there was no wind, but James was still in a gloomy mood. He told Miss Roper to send flowers to Fiona.

'What message?' she asked. And he snapped back.

'Just "Love from James".'

He got one of her shrewd, dry looks. 'Don't look at me like that!' he muttered.

'Like what?'

'A good secretary is not supposed to comment on what her boss does!'

'Did I say a word?'

'You looked volumes—whole dictionaries of words.'

'If I go around staring at the ground I'll trip over.'

'Oh, get out, and send those flowers!'

'Yes, sir. Certainly sir.' She closed his door extra quietly, making his teeth meet.

Lunching with clients, he had to keep dragging his mind back to the subject they were discussing; his mind had a new, worrying tendency to wander away from anything to do with work. What the hell's the matter with you? he asked himself furiously that afternoon, finding himself doodling a face on his blotter. Big eyes, a wide, warm mouth... James scribbled blackly all over it and put down his pen. He would not, must not think about Patience Kirby or her hazel eyes. What colour were they exactly? Hard to be sure; yellowy, greeny, blue. Like opals, the colour seemed to change in different lights, and they had an opalescent flash when she got angry.

Will you stop thinking about her? he told himself, picking up a company balance sheet and forcing himself to concentrate. Maybe he was in need of a holiday? Yes, that was probably it. He buzzed for Miss Roper.

'I think I'll take a few days off soon—check my appointments and let me know the best time for me to go away.'

Her eyes had that omniscient, amused smile. What was she reading into this sudden decision to take time off? Adding two and two and making a hundred, no doubt!

He glared at her. 'That will be all, thank you, Miss Roper.'

'Yes, sir.'

Demurely she sidled out and James drummed his fingertips on his desk, trying not to look at his watch. It was nowhere near time to go home. He still had a couple of dry-as-dust hours to go yet.

On Tuesday his lunch engagement was cancelled at the last minute; the sun had come out, so James took a taxi to the nearest department store, had a salad lunch there, then explored the various departments idly, with no particular motive in mind. It was just a way of filling in time, he told himself, looking at expensive French perfume. He chose a fragrance which seemed very familiar; was he imagining it or had his mother worn it when he was a child? Or something similar; he was hardly an expert but the smell definitely rang bells from long ago.

'Has this perfume been around long?' he asked the assistant, who nodded.

'It was created in the fifties, I think.'

'I thought it was familiar.'

'Oh, a lot of ladies buy it, sir.'

It seemed a good idea to buy two bottles. Just because he'd bought her a present that didn't commit him to going to her party. *Their* party! Patience had been born on the same day; wasn't that an extraordinary coincidence? He couldn't buy his mother a present and not buy Patience one. In the circumstances, as she had invited him to her birthday party, he couldn't turn up empty-handed, could he? She had been very kind to his mother; it was only polite to buy her a bottle of perfume. It meant nothing.

Walking past a display of long, delicate, exquisite georgette scarves in sky-blue, almond-green and pale rose, he picked out two in different colours. Green for his mother, rose for Patience; it was the exact colour of her mouth.

The store wrapped the gifts for him; he wrote out the cards to be taped to the parcels. That reminded him of birthday cards; he took his time choosing them, and wrote inside each and addressed them while he was drinking coffee before leaving the store.

Surprisingly, he had enjoyed his lunch hour more than he usually did; instead of long, tedious meals with businessmen he had been having fun. It was ages since he had had such a good time. Maybe giving presents was good for you?

The London streets sparkled with sunlight as he went back to the office. People were smiling today, not running along with heads bent, faces grim. Spring was definitely here, and James didn't feel much like going back to work, but habit won; he was behind his desk again that afternoon. The presents were locked into a drawer of his desk; he didn't look at them again but they were on his mind—should he send them over by messenger?

By Wednesday he was in a state of permanent dither. To go or not to go? That was the question on James's mind, and he swung from one decision to another all day.

Indecision made him irritable; he knew he was being grumpy. Miss Roper kept giving him those dry, sardonic looks of hers, and the little blonde girl was in a permanent state of jumpiness because he had snapped at her once or twice. Once or twice an hour, all day, he bleakly conceded. Poor girl, it wasn't her fault; he knew he was making her so nervous she couldn't help dropping things and getting messages wrong.

Trying to lighten the mood, James smiled at her, and she immediately dropped the pile of letters she had brought him to sign.

James roared. 'For God's sake, you halfwit, can't you do anything right?'

Miss Roper zoomed in to take over, despatched her whimpering assistant to her own office, picked up the letters and told James coldly, 'If you didn't shout, she wouldn't be so nervous, Mr Ormond.'

'I wasn't shouting when she came in—I smiled, and that only seemed to make her worse!'

'I expect she was afraid you were about to sack her. You usually smile a lot when you're firing people.'

Horrified, James said, 'What on earth do you mean? Are you implying that I enjoy sacking people?'

'I know you don't. That's why you smile; it's pure nerves.' Miss Roper studied him. 'What are you nervous about now?'

James began signing the letters without answering. If there was one thing he could not stand it was women who thought they could read his mind.

When Barny came to pick him up he had the parcels with him, inside the bag the department store had given him. Miss Roper eyed the bag curiously, reading the logo on the side with obvious interest as James said goodnight, but didn't comment, perhaps because James's eyes dared her to try!

As Barny started the engine James said, 'Not home, Barny—Muswell Hill, please.'

Barny did a double-take, staring round at him. James leaned back and gazed fixedly out of the window at the city street crowded with home-going workers.

After a few seconds Barny set off without asking any questions. It was quite a long drive north, through London, to the hilly suburb. Staring out at busy, unfamiliar streets, James found his eye caught by something in a pet shop window.

'Stop!' he urgently told Barny, who pulled over into a small car park in front of the line of shops.

James jumped out. 'I won't be long.' He dashed into the pet shop and a few moments later emerged with a Victorian-style bird cage, painted white, in which some yellow birds hopped and sang.

Barny eyed them with uncertainty. 'Taken to keeping birds, have you?'

'No, they're a present.' James climbed into the back

of the car and put the cage down on the floor. 'Okay, off we go again.'

Over his shoulder Barny murmured, 'Not everyone likes birds, you know. Messy little things in a house, chucking seed around. Noisy, too, especially first thing in the morning.'

'I can always take them back.' It had been an impulse buy; James hoped he hadn't done the wrong thing.

As they turned into the road where Patience lived James felt an odd reverberation inside his chest like the rumble of a coming earthquake. It was just as well Miss Roper wasn't there to give him one of her omniscient smiles.

'Do you want me to wait for you?' Barny asked as he pulled up outside The Cedars.

'No, I'll call a taxi. I hope you and Enid have a nice evening with your friends.' They were going to a party given by a couple they had known for years, their closest friends, who had a café near the British Museum now but had once worked for a family living next door to James. Barny and Enid had often said wistfully that one day they would like to have a café or a boarding-house, but they had stayed on because Enid didn't like to leave James alone with strangers.

Thinking of that, James smiled, and Barny smiled back.

'I hope you have a good evening too. Give our best wishes to the young lady.'

James felt himself go red and knew Barny noticed; he could have kicked himself. Why did he keep doing that?

He got out of the car and slammed the door with his foot because his hands were full—a bag in one, the bird cage in the other. Before he walked away Barny said, 'And our love to Madam—her birthday, isn't it?'

Stopping as if shot in his tracks, James swung back. 'How do you know that?'

Barny was unflappable as ever, meeting his eyes openly, seriously. 'Enid remembered. A great one for birthdays, Enid, never forgets anyone's.'

James smiled. 'She never forgot mine.' And his father had never remembered it. 'Goodnight, Barny.'

He could hear the noise of the party long before he reached the house, and paused on the drive to listen to the voices and laughter, the dogs barking, the sound of music. It sounded as if they were all having a marvellous time.

The trees breathed all round him, and the scent of spring was in the air from the daffodils and hyacinths he could not see; above the roof of the house the night sky flowed, deep blue, clear and cloudless.

He had to ring four times before the front door finally opened and a host of children and dogs rushed out. Emmy got to him first, flinging her arms around the nearest part of him she could reach, hugging his waist.

'I knew you'd come! I've been listening for the doorbell for ages; you're late.' Then she looked down at the bird cage and gave a loud gasp of delight. 'Birds! They're lovely—are they for me?'

Over her head he met Patience's eyes and helplessly said, 'I saw them in a pet shop window on the way here and thought she…the children…might like them.'

Emmy took the metal loop off his fingers and put both arms around the cage to support it, peering through the bars at the birds, who flew anxiously around from perch to perch.

'It's too heavy for you; I'll carry it,' Toby said, forcefully removing the cage from her.

'Give them back, they're mine!' yelled Emmy, grabbing.

Toby fended her off with his elbow. 'You might drop the cage and kill the birds; don't be stupid. What are they, James? Canaries?'

'Yes,' James said abstractedly, watching Emmy's tears well up. 'Don't cry, Emmy. There's one each for all three of you, and you can choose first.'

'Who's looking after them?' Patience demanded sternly, eying the children. 'And that means feeding them regularly, cleaning out their cage, checking on their claws and beaks and feathers once a week—it doesn't just mean playing with them.'

'Me!' Emmy said.

The boys laughed. 'In a pig's eye! I'll do it, and she can help me,' Toby said, carrying the cage indoors with the others following. The dogs rushed after them, barking excitedly at the birds, who hopped and twittered in agitation.

'Shh...shh...bad dogs,' Emmy scolded them as the little party disappeared.

'Are you coming in or not?' Patience asked him, her face glimmering softly in the faint light.

He just stared down at her without answering. Silence enveloped them, but not an uncomfortable silence; he did not feel the need to speak, nor, apparently, did she. It seemed a lifetime since he last saw her; it also seemed like the mere blink of an eye.

His chest contracted; he could hardly breathe. Is this falling in love? he thought. Is this how it feels? This dizziness, this intense concentration on one other human being—is this love? His eyes absorbed the tendrils of bright hair on her forehead, the wide eyes shining like a cat's in the dark, the slightly parted lips, as if she might smile at any minute.

It would be so easy to love her. Panic shot through him like fire through a house; he felt himself burning up, lost for ever.

He couldn't let it happen. He was too old for her. They came from such different places, worlds that never met. He moved in a world of ruthless drive, cold calculation, where the bottom line was always money and nothing mattered but success. Her world was based on family and warmth, love and duty; for her what mattered was always going to be people. If those two worlds collided it could only lead to pain, even destruction, for one or other of them, if not both.

It would be madness even to contemplate it—and he had always prided himself on being very sane.

What was he doing here? He shouldn't have come. Angry with himself more than with her, he burst out, 'I hope you're satisfied now. I came—but only because you used emotional blackmail. Well, it won't work twice. I am not seeing my mother again after this. I'll make her a decent allowance so that she can live comfortably, but there is no place for her in my life, is that understood?'

CHAPTER FIVE

'YOU'VE got a horrible temper,' Patience said. 'No need to shout at me. I'm not your conscience.'

'No, you're damned well not! So stop trying to make me feel guilty.'

She gave James one of those maddening stares, half smiling that little Mona Lisa smile of hers, her eyes bright with mockery, or amusement.

'I'm not trying to make you feel anything. Whatever you feel is entirely down to you.' She turned to go back inside and he caught her wrist to stop her, swinging her round.

Off balance, she collided with him and his whole body tensed with reaction. For a second he really believed she was going to fall over; instinctively he put his other arm round her waist to support her, and the warmth of her flesh came through the thin, gauzy blue and green dress she was wearing, making a strange shiver run through him. He stared down at the scooped neckline which almost showed the rise of her small breasts, the tight sashed waist, the full, spreading skirt. The way the soft material clung to her made his mouth go dry.

This close he was breathing the scented air around her, the faint, delicate perfume in her fiery red hair, all over her slight body. He bent his head, as if stooping to smell a flower, and felt the warmth of her cheek against his.

His splayed fingers slowly moved down from her waist, with James only half aware of what he was doing, stroking and caressing the small buttocks, pushing her towards him while his lips slid sideways, hunting for her mouth. He had to kiss her. Had to.

She didn't fight him, yielded wordlessly, her body bending under his fingers as if she were plastic, her lips softly parting as he kissed her. James shut his eyes and let himself fall into the warm, breathing darkness of the night, his mind as closed as his eyes, everything alive in him concentrated on the sensation of touching her, holding her, kissing her.

It was only at that instant that he admitted how much he had been wanting to do this ever since he set eyes on her, but before he could face his own emotions the intense pleasure of that moment was shattered abruptly when someone exploded out of the house and leapt on him, pulling him away from Patience. A fist crashed into his face. James was still dazed from that kiss. He went over backwards, fell out into the drive in a dramatic sprawl, not even sure what had happened to him, only knowing that his cheekbone was throbbing, the back of his head was hurting and somewhere Patience was yelling.

'What did you do that for, you idiot?'

'Why did you let him kiss you?'

'Oh, don't be such a prat, Col!'

'I knew he was after you the minute I saw him.'

A brief pause, then Patience said, 'What do you mean? Why did you think he...?'

'Fancied you? Of course he does—it was obvious. I saw the way he looked at you.'

The boy sounded explosive but Patience was calm, almost reflective, as if thinking over what he was saying. 'How did he look at me?'

'You know what I mean! He never takes his eyes off

you; don't tell me you hadn't noticed—you're not blind. But he's so old! My God, Patience, he could be your father!'

'Don't be ridiculous; he's only about ten years older than me.'

'Much more than that—fifteen, I'd say!' The boy's voice broke, as if he was about to cry. 'Oh, Patience, how could you let him kiss you like that?'

'Col, can't you get it into your head? I'm not your property; I don't have to ask your permission before I let someone kiss me.'

'You're my girl; you know you are! You never go out with anyone else.'

'I never have time to meet anyone else, do I? I'm too busy. I haven't had a chance to look around, experiment.'

'Was that what you were doing just now? Experimenting? You can't have liked it; you can't have done!'

The breathless, shaking young voice was only too familiar—Colin something or other, the boy he had seen briefly last time he was here. She had said the boy was aggressive; she hadn't exaggerated. The fist which had collided with his face had had more power behind it than James would have expected from that skinny boy's body. Humiliating to be knocked down by a teenager half his age. Thank God there had been no other witnesses. Bad enough that Patience had seen it.

Having got his breath back, and able to think clearly again, James began to get back on his feet just as Patience rushed out to help him.

'Are you okay?'

'It took you a long time to wonder about that, didn't it?' he snarled, brushing gravel off his previously immaculate trousers. 'I could have been dead for all the interest you took. The only thing you wanted to do was quarrel with your boyfriend.'

'Don't shout at me! It wasn't me who hit you!' she said, not denying that Colin was her boyfriend. But then she couldn't, could she? Not with that boy listening.

His jaws tight, James muttered, 'I know who it was!' and turned furious eyes on the boy. 'And he isn't getting away with it. He hit me before I had a chance to know what was coming; he won't be so lucky next time.'

'We'll see about that!' Colin yelled.

She got between them. No doubt she was worried about what he might do to the boy, and she had every right to be worried, even if the boy had knocked him down a moment ago. He had caught James off balance and now James wanted to do something violent; he was seeing everything through a red haze of rage.

'Oh, don't you be stupid too!' she said with a heavy sigh, as if they were both children and she was the only adult in sight. 'I didn't expect that from you. You're old enough to know better.'

Did she have to keep emphasising his age?

'I'm not drawing my old-age pension yet!' he snapped, but she was looking at the boy, not him, and wasn't interested in anything he had to say—which made James even angrier.

'Colin, tell Mr Ormond you're sorry,' she ordered, and the boy's jaw dropped. James heard him gasp with affront.

'No, I won't! I'm not sorry I hit him. The only thing I'm sorry about is that I didn't hit him harder.'

'Try it again and you will be sorry!' James threatened, knowing he was being as big a fool as this boy, yet unable to stop himself.

The boy put up his fists like a boxer and danced about, ready for a fight. 'Come on, then—I'm not scared of you.'

Patience smacked his hands down. 'Go home, Colin!'

He looked as if he might burst into tears any minute, staring at her as if he didn't believe his ears. 'But your party! Are you saying I can't come to your birthday party?'

'Not if you can't behave yourself like a grown-up. I won't have you fighting Mr Ormond; it would ruin my birthday.'

'Then send him away, not me! Who wants him here, anyway?'

'His mother does—it's her birthday, too, remember!' Her tone softened and she smiled at Colin. 'You like Mrs Ormond, don't you? You don't want to upset her on her birthday.'

James watched the two of them, his teeth grating. Why did she waste her warm, gentle smile on that gangling boy who was far too young to appreciate it?

At that moment Emmy came running back, blithely oblivious of any atmosphere between the adults. 'Aren't you coming in, James? Come on, we're all waiting for you. You didn't notice my new dress. Isn't it pretty?'

He bent to kiss her cheek. 'Very pretty. It suits you.' He meant it, too. Just the sight of her made his heart lift. Her dress was bright pink taffeta and should have clashed horribly with her red hair, but somehow it didn't; she looked adorable, with her wide sash which floated down the back in two streamers over her full skirts.

Obviously he had said the right thing because she beamed, her whole face lighting up. 'It's new. I never wore it before. Listen...' She did a little dance and her skirts flew around her, rustling noisily at every move. 'Isn't that great?'

'Great. I love it, and I love the way you've done your hair.' It had been tied into two curly bunches with matching pink ribbons and her cheeks were pink, too, with excitement.

'Your mother made the dress for her; it was very kind of her to take so much trouble,' Patience said.

'Ruth told me I could have any colour I liked. Patience took me to the shop and I picked pink. I love pink.'

'Huh! You look like a pink blancmange, all fat and wobbly,' Tom insulted, arriving.

Emmy whirled round to rush at Tom and hit out at him with both of her dimpled, screwed up fists. Tom shoved her away effortlessly and she tumbled back into James, who picked her up, frowning sternly at Tom, shaking his head.

'You shouldn't hit girls.' He caught a look of sarcasm in Patience's eyes and flushed slightly, remembering the first time they'd met, when he'd ordered his security men to carry her out of the building. He knew that that was what she was thinking about; her hazel eyes were eloquent.

It was odd, he was beginning to be able to read her mind, but then her small face was so expressive that every thought she had showed in her luminous eyes and the fleeting movements of her full mouth.

'She hit me first,' protested Tom indignantly.

'You were rude about her—what do you expect?' James avoided meeting Patience's gaze, wishing she would stop looking as if everything he said amused her.

'I don't look like a blancmange, do I?' Emmy asked him, and James shook his head.

'Of course not, you look beautiful.' Over her curly head he met Patience's eyes with a cold, forbidding stare. Let her laugh at that! But she didn't; she smiled at him and his chest constricted as if in pain or pleasure so extreme that it made his heart hurt. That wonderful warm smile had been all for him that time, and it was like being handed a rainbow.

He couldn't remember anyone in his life who had had a smile like that. When Fiona smiled it was just a movement of her elegant mouth; it held no real warmth— courtesy sometimes, sensuality at times, yes, mockery quite often, but not warmth. He was only just beginning to realise how little warmth there had ever been in his life and how much he had always needed some without being aware of it.

'It's getting cold out here. Come on, the party food is already laid out; supper is ready,' Patience said to James.

The children ran ahead. Colin sullenly said to Patience, 'What about me? Can I come or not?'

'First apologise to Mr Ormond for hitting him.'

Colin growled, 'Oh, forget it! I don't want to come, anyway, if he's going to be here.'

He rushed away down the drive and Patience gave a little sigh. 'Oh, dear. Now he'll sulk for days.' Looking at James, she asked him, 'Did Colin hurt you much?'

He felt his cheekbone. 'It's just a bruise.'

'I'll put something on it in a minute,' she promised.

Picking up his two packages, James followed her into the house, watching the grace with which she moved in the vivid green and blue muslin dress which fell to mid-calf, fluttering around her slender legs. She looked like spring, with her sunny hair.

'Your dress is very pretty, too,' he told her huskily, and she looked back over her shoulder, smiling.

At that odd angle her face came very close to beauty, the delicate geometry of cheek and eye and temple revealed and then gone again as she turned away once more.

'Your mother again,' she said. 'I usually wear jeans, as you've probably noticed; they're cheaper and more hard-wearing than anything else. I have to be practical—I have so much to do. When your mother found out that I didn't have anything new to wear for the party she insisted on making this for me; it's my birthday present from her.'

'I had no idea she was good at sewing.' But then, what *did* he know about her? Her life was a blank to him; they were strangers. How could she expect him to treat her as anything else after all these years?

'She uses our old sewing machine; it was amazing that she could get it to work at all, it had been up in the attic for ages, but Joe is a whizz with machinery of any kind. He oiled it and mended it, and she has been busy with it ever since, making things for everyone. She seems to be enjoying doing the work, too.

'She can't stand up for long, or move about easily. And she has such bad arthritis she has to work slowly and carefully, because her hands are often very swollen, but I think the exercise is good for her knuckles—they get worse if she doesn't use her hands at all, and it makes her feel better to be doing something instead of just sitting about in a chair reading or listening to music or watching TV.

'I encourage them all to have a hobby: painting or growing house plants or making homemade wine. It's good for them to do their own thing and be independent. It's nice to have company, to have other people around, but sometimes everyone needs to be alone.'

'What about you? How much time alone do you get?'

She grimaced, laughing. 'Not a lot!'

They arrived in the crowded dining room and everyone at the table looked up and smiled, greeting him. He smiled back and said, 'Hallo, how are you all?' feeling very self-conscious after the way he had left this house last time he was here. He knew by now how much they all talked and gossiped; they all knew about him and his mother. They probably all knew he had slammed out of this house last time he came.

But their faces gave nothing away; they looked very friendly as they all chorused, 'Hallo!'

The children were not sitting at the table; they had placed the bird cage on the old oak sideboard behind them, beside a huge bowl of fresh fruit and a pile of plates. The canaries were singing away cheerfully and, he noted ruefully, chucking bird seed about.

'I hope those birds aren't going to be too much of a nuisance for you,' he said uneasily to Patience.

'They're marvellous—aren't they, gang?' She smiled at everyone around the table, who all nodded.

'Very pretty,' said one old lady. 'And I like to hear them twittering like that; it makes the room feel cheerful.'

'I've got a couple of budgies up in my room,' said Lavinia, 'You should hear them! Talk a blue streak, they do, and not all of it fit for polite company, because my husband taught them to speak and he was inclined to swear if he lost his temper. What amazes me is that he's been dead two years but those birds still remember what they learnt from him.'

'You can talk to birds; you can't talk to fishes,' said Joe.

'I do,' said Toby.

'Do they talk back?' Joe teased him, amused to see him go red.

Toby glared. 'Of course not, but they always come up to the glass and stare at me.'

'I bet they do. Think you're crackers, I expect! I know I do; talking to fish! You'll be talking to seven-foot-high invisible rabbits next.'

Toby looked blank, never having heard of the famous film *Harvey*, in which a man talks to an invisible white rabbit. 'What are you talking about?'

Joe shrugged. 'Oh, never mind.'

'You're sitting by me,' Emmy called, and James squeezed round the other side of the table to take the empty chair. It was only as he sat down that he realised his mother was sitting on the other side of him.

He flushed and she said, 'Thank you for coming, James. I was afraid you wouldn't and I'm so glad you did.'

He didn't know what to say, but luckily he remembered the packages he held and pushed the one topped with a green silk bow towards her. 'Happy Birthday.'

Everyone stopped talking to watch. Pink and surprised, Ruth Ormond fumbled with the parcel, and it was only at that second that James noticed that her knuckles were gnarled and swollen with arthritis, as Patience had told him a moment ago. He hadn't looked at her hands closely enough to see that the last time he came; he had been too busy observing that she no longer wore rings, as she had done when he was a child.

'Let me do that,' he said, taking the parcel and deftly opening it for her before pushing it back to her.

She took out the bottle of perfume first, in the famous black and gold packaging. Her eyes lifted to her son's face, bright with unshed tears. 'You remembered my favourite perfume! I haven't worn this for years; I couldn't afford luxuries like this.'

He was startled; surely he had smelt it in her room the other day when he came here? He couldn't have imagined it!

Realising that she was trying now to open the box, he leaned over and did that for her, freed with some difficulty the stopper, and watched her invert the bottle then use the stopper to dab some of the perfume behind her ears and at her wrists. The scent entered his nostrils and he gave a barely audible sigh. Yes, that was what he had smelt when he walked into his mother's room and saw her. How extraordinary the human mind was! His memory and imagination had instantly combined to make him believe he could smell the perfume she had always worn in his childhood. A mental conjuring trick.

Inhaling the scent, his mother sighed. 'Oh, it's so wonderful to smell it again.' She held out her wrist to him. 'Isn't it gorgeous? Remember it?'

He bent to inhale the scent, then straightened, nodding. 'Yes, I remember.' That was the perfume he had always associated with her in his mind; that was why he had believed he smelt it when he'd walked into her room.

'There's something else in the parcel,' Emmy pointed out, bending to peer inside the wrapping.

James unwrapped the scarf; Emmy gave a little gasp of delight. 'Oh, that's lovely!'

Ruth Ormond's face lit up. She held the silky green scarf between her gnarled hands, lifted it to her cheek. 'Oh, how pretty. I love that colour. I'll wear it now.'

James stood up, taking the scarf from her, and flung it lightly around her shoulders. His mother stroked down the long folds against the pale pink dress she wore.

'Thank you, James, I love both my presents.'

'Oh, I forgot your card,' he said, handing that to her, and then sat down again while she opened it, studied the picture on the front and then looked at his scrawled name inside.

Emmy was staring at the other package on the table in front of him. 'Who is that for?'

Everyone else stared, too. His colour rising, James cleared his throat. 'Oh, yes, I forgot...' He looked across the table at Patience. 'Happy Birthday.' He pushed the package towards her.

She looked startled. 'Oh, You shouldn't...didn't have to... I mean, thank you, that's very kind.' For once, he was glad to see, he had taken her by surprise and made her lose her cool. Usually it was he who was at a disadvantage; he was pleased to turn the tables.

'Open it, Patience!' Emmy urged.

She carefully undid the parcel, took out the perfume and stared at it. 'Heavens.'

'It's the same as Ruth's!' Emmy was always ready to point out the obvious.

James was flushed. 'I'm afraid I don't have much imagination. If you don't like it I can always take it back and change it, if you'd rather have another perfume? I didn't know what perfume you liked.'

She took the stopper out of the bottle and lifted it, breathed in the scent from it, her eyes half-closed. 'Mmm...marvellous.' She smiled across the table, her hazel eyes very bright. 'I've never had any French perfume before; it costs too much for me so I'm thrilled. It's wonderful—thank you. I love it.'

'There's a scarf for you, too,' he confessed. 'I chose pink for you. I told you I didn't have much imagination.' Then his eyes lifted to observe her vivid red hair—

maybe he should have given his mother the pink and given Patience green?

She held the delicate silky folds in her hands, gazing at them. 'What a gorgeous colour. That was very clever of you, James—how did you know I loved pink but never dare risk wearing it? People with red hair aren't supposed to wear pink, so nobody's ever bought me pink before, and I don't often buy myself anything as pretty as this because it would soon be ruined if I wore it when I was working—which I nearly always am!' She looked down at her green and blue dress uncertainly. 'Do you think I could wear it with this dress?'

Beside him, Emmy gave a deep sigh of envy. 'Of course you can. It will look lovely—just like rose petals—I bet it feels nice when you wear it, too.'

Patience wound it around her throat twice, then let the rest of it float down behind her back. 'How does it look, Em?'

'Oh, lovely.'

'Honestly?'

'Promise—cross my heart, hope to die. I don't care what anyone says; I love pink with red hair.'

'So do I.'

They were looking at each other intently across the table, sisters in every sense of the word, the child and the young woman united in their serious contemplation of one of the more important matters in life.

Patience looked across the table at James. 'What do you think?'

'You look wonderful; it exactly matches your lipstick,' he said, and halfway through the sentence was terrified that his voice betrayed how he felt whenever he looked at that wide, warm, invitingly pink mouth.

As he stared it curved into a smile which he watched

like someone watching the sun come up, remembering the way her mouth had felt under his when he kissed her earlier.

'When are we going to start eating?' growled Tom.

'Yes, I'm starving,' Joe said crossly.

'You can say grace, Joe,' Patience told him, with one of her teasing little grins.

'Me? Do I have to? Should be you; it's your birthday. Or Ruth.' Joe had that mutinous look he had when he was about to dig his toes in.

Ruth Ormond said grace before Patience could start an argument with Joe, and everyone reached for one of the plates of tiny triangular sandwiches filled with cucumber, tomato or thin sliced cheese.

'What are these meant to be? One bite and they're gone,' grumbled Joe, eating three at once.

'They're meant to be elegant. Don't gobble, we haven't brought all the food in yet,' Lavinia scolded, hurrying out to the kitchen.

She brought in hot buttered crumpets and muffins; there were two for everyone, although Joe ate three, but as Emmy only ate one that didn't matter.

The food kept coming—sausage rolls, Scotch eggs, which James loved because the mixture of hard-boiled eggs wrapped in sausagemeat which was coated in bread crumbs and fried was something Enid did particularly well and often served with salad, and there were sweet things, too, of course: red and orange jelly, banana blancmange and strawberry trifle, chocolate finger biscuits and small cakes. The party ended when they lit the candles on the large birthday cake on top of which Lavinia had written 'HAPPY BIRTHDAY' in pink icing. Patience and Ruth Ormond blew the candles out together, in one long blow, and everyone sang 'Happy Birthday' to them.

Emmy had contributed an oddly shaped blue marzipan rabbit and a yellow marzipan banana which she had arranged on top of the cake.

'Which one do I eat?' James's mother asked.

'The banana's nice,' Emmy ingenuously said.

'Oh, yes, I'd eat the banana,' James recommended, not confident that the blue marzipan of the rabbit would be very palatable, anyway. It looked eerie, like something from outer space.

Emmy beamed as Ruth took the banana. 'Mmm, delicious,' Ruth said, nibbling at it.

'I couldn't eat another thing,' Patience said. 'You have the rabbit, Emmy.'

Smiling even wider, Emmy ate the rabbit while her brothers regarded her with disgust.

'You know Patience hates marzipan!' Toby told her, but she ignored him, biting off the ears last with her eyes half shut.

'I love it,' Ruth Ormond said hurriedly, finishing her marzipan banana.

After tea they had party games—Pin the Tail on the Donkey, Oranges and Lemons, which the old people played at a stately pace, laughing all the time, and Pass the Parcel, a game which Joe cheated at and managed to win. So he got the contents of the parcel—a box of chocolates—but Lavinia and the others were highly indignant.

Ruth Ormond went to bed a few minutes later. 'It's been a wonderful day; I think I just ran out of energy!' she said to her son.

James could see she was pale under her make-up and

frowned, realising just how frail she was. 'Can you manage the stairs?'

She nodded, smiling, and bent, suddenly, to kiss his cheek. 'Goodnight. Thank you for my presents, James.'

Patience went with her; James followed them into the hall and asked, 'May I ring for a taxi? I really should be going.'

'Help yourself.' Patience nodded.

He had finished his call when she came back a few minutes later.

'Is she okay?' James asked, and was surprised to realise he was anxious.

'Tired, but fine. She's had a lovely day, and the highlight was you turning up. She was afraid you wouldn't.'

'I nearly didn't.' He turned dark red, all the old pain and rage welling up in him again. 'After all, why should I? What can she expect? She walked out on me when I was ten years old, just swanned off with some guy, leaving me behind with a father who was as cold as ice, knowing I was going to get a miserable childhood with him! How dare she just turn up again now, twenty-five years later, and ask me to forgive and forget?'

Impatiently, Patience said, 'But you aren't a little boy any more, you're a man, and it was all a long, long time ago! You must have got over it by now, and poor Ruth is very lonely; she's old and sick and needs you.'

'She forfeited her right to be my mother all those years ago—her choice, not mine.'

'Give her a second chance, James!'

'Why should I?' James felt suffocated, his pain and anger was so intense. Hoarsely, he muttered, 'What right has she to turn up in my life and make emotional demands after all this time?'

Patience was looking at him in a way he bitterly resented. He had no difficulty reading everything in that mobile face: contempt, condemnation, coldness.

'Stupid of her to think she could,' she said icily. 'You can't get blood out of a stone, and you can't get emotion from a man who lives in an emotional refrigerator! But then Ruth is very old and afraid of dying, and she's clinging to a dream. I'm sorry for her, and I don't want to hurt her, or I'd tell her to forget it because you're never going to be human enough to forgive her. I don't think there's anything human inside you.'

Rage clawed inside James like a wild cat imprisoned in his chest. He was breathing thickly, couldn't speak, his hands clenched into fists, his eyes smouldering as they stared down at her. She had no right to speak to him like that. Was that what she thought of him, then? That he wasn't human? That he lived in a refrigerator?

Honesty compelled him to admit that he had done for most of his life, yes. His father had locked him up there years ago. But lately... He flinched away from admitting what had been happening to him lately. Since the day Patience had erupted into his office everything in his life had altered. But he had been a fool to get so involved with a girl who was far too young for him and, anyway, already had a boyfriend of her own age.

He would be stupid not to recognise that Patience had been using him, trying to manipulate him, taking advantage of the attraction she must have realised he felt. Oh, no doubt she told herself that she was justified, that it was all in a good cause—she wanted to help his mother and, being a woman, it came naturally to her to be devious and ruthless, to use his own weakness against him.

He looked into her hazel eyes bitterly, and found them staring back with just as much anger.

And she didn't even really like him! He had been

trying to convince himself she did, but that was dislike in her face! She despised him.

The idea was painful. He had never cared whether or not people disliked him. That was something else he had begun to do—care about people. A few weeks ago he would have called himself strong-minded, tough, self-confident. Now he knew he had weaknesses which could destroy him if he didn't do something about them, fast.

'Perhaps you'll stop bothering me now, then!' he snapped at Patience, who glared back.

'Don't worry, I'll never bother you again!'

They were so furiously intent on each other that they both jumped when the taxi arrived outside and hooted sharply.

Patience took a long breath. 'Goodbye.' Her voice was tart, and as cold as the north wind.

James wrenched himself away, pulled open the front door and walked very fast down the drive to where the taxi was waiting. He gave the driver his address and leaned back without looking at the house again as he was driven off into the night and headed southwards into central London.

That was the last time he would ever go there; he would never see Patience again, he told himself, and felt something sharp and agonising jab deep inside his chest.

'Never' was a desert in which he had been abandoned when he was ten years old; his mother had vanished and his father had told him he would never see her again. Now it was happening to him again; he was back in that bleak, empty landscape—only this time he was doing it to himself.

CHAPTER SIX

A WEEK or so later James ran into Fiona at a reception given by a large American banking institution which had an office in the City of London. Once upon a time most of the guests would have been men, but today women occupied very important jobs in the City, and it did not surprise James to see Fiona across the other side of the room. She was talking to several much older men who couldn't take their eyes off her. She looked like a blonde Cleopatra, her sinuous figure emphasised by a skintight black dress, her mouth darkly red, her eyelids glittering with silvery blue shadow and outlined in thick black.

James was talking to one of his clients, but from time to time he checked on where Fiona was, wondering whether to go over to her or let her come to him. Tactically, the latter would be preferable. He was in no mood to let any woman think she could jerk his string and have him come running.

Ever since he'd walked out of Patience's house he had been irritable, depressed, moody. He knew everyone had noticed; Barny and Enid kept giving him sideways looks, Miss Roper was warily observant every time he opened his mouth, and the little blonde airhead was in a constant state of panic for which James refused to be held responsible. Since she was now wearing an engagement ring on one hand—which, of course, had meant she and Miss Roper, and most of the female secretarial staff, disappearing for a long lunch break the other day, to celebrate her new status as an engaged person—he had hoped some unfortunate man was about to marry her and rid his office of her for good. Miss Roper had disabused him of this hope, though.

'They aren't getting married until next year and she isn't giving up work. Good heavens, people can't afford to stop work these days just because they get married. I expect she'll stop when she has a baby, but she doesn't plan to have one for a few years.'

'Very wise. She's hardly capable of making coffee, let alone looking after a baby,' James said, and got one of Miss Roper's dry looks.

'You need a holiday,' she said, adding, 'Sir!' in a voice that stung like a wasp, and laid on his desk a typed list. 'You asked me to check a time when you could take a few days off without causing too much of a problem. I'm afraid you have a busy schedule for the next month, but if you delegated…'

'No, I've changed my mind. I can't take any time off yet.'

'May would be a good time to take a week off. You don't have too many appointments in the first week, and you could reschedule those you do have.'

He stared at the typed sheet. 'I'll think about it.'

But he hadn't. Maybe he would go abroad, spend a week on a beach somewhere, just sunbathing and forgetting about work? About his mother and Patience Kirby, too. He had been trying to forget them for days now but they ran round and round inside his head like white mice on a turning wheel. Not that anyone could be less like a mouse, white or otherwise, than Patience, with her red hair and her wide, enchanting mouth, and those teasing, bright hazel eyes. She had a colour and warmth that blazed, was unforgettable.

'Hallo, James.'

He had been so absorbed in images of Patience that Fiona's melting ice-cream voice took him by surprise.

'Oh...hello, Fiona,' he said blankly, then pulled himself together. 'You look marvellous—what an elegant dress; black suits you. Very dramatic.' Did he sound as insincere as he felt? He was having to force the words out, yet it was true; she did look terrific and black did suit her. She was born to wear it with that very fair skin and fair hair.

She smiled, her long, darkened lashes sweeping down against her smooth skin. 'Thank you. How are you? It must be a long time since our last date.'

'Ages,' he agreed. 'But you did tell me you were going to be very busy while your father was away. When does he get back from his trip?'

'He got back this morning.'

'How did the trip go? Did he enjoy himself?'

She brushed aside the question of enjoyment with a wry little smile. 'He was there purely on business. He managed to see everyone he wanted to see, and I think the trip was very successful. He felt it was worthwhile.' Fiona narrowed her eyes at him. 'You don't look too well, James. Anything wrong?'

He had a crazy impulse to tell her the truth, to blurt out: Yes, I'm as miserable as sin. I can't stop losing my temper over nothing, I can't sleep at night, I'm sick of my job. But what if she asked the obvious question: Why? What's wrong? What did he say then?

He shrugged, instead, and pretended to laugh. 'My secretary tells me I'm overworking and need a holiday.'

She watched him closely. 'You do work very long hours, don't you, James? So are you going to take some time off?'

He shook his head. 'Certainly not for a while—I have

a crowded appointment book, no spare time at all for months.'

Fiona nodded. 'Same here.' She looked at her watch. 'Well, I must be off; I'm having dinner with a client. See you, James.'

'We must have dinner, now your father is back,' he quickly said before she could walk away.

She gave him a curious glance through her lashes, lifting her darkened brows as if she did not quite trust what he was saying. 'Love to—give me a ring.' Did she think he was simply making polite noises?

He felt impelled to insist on making a concrete arrangement. 'How about tomorrow night?'

'Tomorrow?' She distinctly hesitated, then said slowly, 'Yes, actually I am free tomorrow.'

'I'll pick you up at seven? Where would you like to eat?'

'You choose.' She looked at her watch again. 'So I'll see you at seven, tomorrow. Sorry, I must rush or I'll be late.'

James watched her cross the room and disappear. He wasn't the only man with his eyes on her; as she passed them men turned their heads to stare at the ice-blonde hair, the arctic blue eyes, the model-girl figure in the tight black dress. She was desirable, and she knew it; her swaying walk was that of a woman who knew men were watching her avidly.

She used her looks without compunction to get what she wanted, and James had always known other men desired her. He remembered what Charles had said only the other day: he'd called him a lucky bastard, he envied him, but then Charles thought he was sleeping with Fiona. Charles would be amazed if he knew the truth.

Fiona was an ice goddess, beautiful but chilly, a hard,

tough woman who could fight as hard as a man in the business world, who was fixated on success and money. That was her sole criterion for judging a man. He had to be rich and powerful or Fiona wasn't interested, even if he was very good-looking.

Had that been the only reason why she had dated him? James thought, frowning. She certainly hadn't felt any overriding desire for him, had she? Or they would have been sleeping together for months. Had she ever had any deep feelings for him at all? Had she ever had any deep feelings for anyone? Or was she cold-hearted, self-obsessed, her sights set on money and power?

What did he know of women, anyway? He didn't understand any of them: Fiona, Patience, his mother, Miss Roper, Enid, even the fluffy-headed little blonde who jumped like a frightened mouse every time she saw him. They were all a mystery to him.

Come to that, he didn't even understand himself. Why had he started seeing Fiona, anyway? He hadn't fallen in love. He had just liked the look of her, had been pleased with himself for getting such a spectacular date, enjoyed the sensation of having other men envy him when he walked into a room with her on his arm. That made him feel ten feet tall, gave his ego a boost.

But he hadn't fallen head over heels, had he? Fiona was well connected, would make an excellent wife for any man who wanted to succeed. She knew a lot of very influential people, she could be charming and smooth in social contexts, she would be a great hostess, give wonderful dinner parties, be a big asset to his career. They had both been as cold-hearted as each other, hadn't they?

So why was he dating her again tomorrow? Ego again? Because she had seemed indifferent, and he wanted to make her regret it if he walked out of her life?

No, not that stupid, or that simple. He was trying to get back to normal, back to the way he had been before…

Before what? He irritably caught himself up. Oh, stop facing the issue, he thought, grinding his teeth so loudly as he left the reception that the porter holding the door open for him gave him a startled, alarmed stare.

James walked over to where Barny was waiting. 'Home, sir?' asked Barny, looking back at him as James climbed into the back of the car and slammed the door behind him.

Nodding, James settled back. What was the issue here, anyway? But he knew perfectly well. Patience was the issue. Before he met Patience his life had been quiet, peaceful, boring.

Oh, don't be ridiculous! How could it have been boring? He had been busy, had a great social life, a terrific future ahead of him, a beautiful girlfriend. What more could any man want? Yes, he had to get that life back. Why shouldn't he?

He groaned aloud, forgetting Barny, his eyes closed, knowing that he was a drowning man trying to grab at straws. Fiona was the straw he was clutching at, but he knew even as he grabbed at her that she wouldn't save him. He didn't care enough about her to be rescued. He was going to drown in deep, black waters of loneliness and isolation, with or without Fiona.

'Toothache, sir?' Barny asked.

With a start James opened his eyes, shook his head, frowning. 'No, just thinking.' Couldn't he even think without being watched and commented on?

Barny refrained from comment on that, but softly murmured, 'So we aren't going up to Muswell Hill tonight, then?'

James glared murderously. 'No, we are not! We are never going there again.'

Barny distinctly said, 'Ah.'

'"Ah", what?' snarled James.

'I didn't say anything, sir,' Barny lied, and a few moments later they were in Regent's Park and James stamped off into the house without another word.

He stood in his bedroom that evening, the curtains open, staring out into the darkness of the park, hearing the distant roar of a lion, the chattering of monkeys swinging around their cages, the flap of many wings, all the night-time sounds that came out through the trees, as if these elegant, exclusive streets which curled round and round like the maze of a human ear held the jungle hidden within them.

As a small child he remembered a welling fear, the uncertainty of someone who didn't feel safe any more, who was alone and lost and yet afraid to cry. He had been afraid the animals would one day get out and hunt him, tear him to pieces; he had imagined them loping through the streets with people running in all directions, screaming in fear. Life had been a jungle to him all his life. Maybe he would never feel safe.

Shivering at that idea, he turned away, drew the curtains, got undressed and went to bed, knowing even as he turned out the light that he wouldn't sleep, or, if he did, would have dark dreams that made him feel exhausted next morning.

Red rims around his eyes, his temper in shreds, he went into work next day and gave his staff hell, knowing what he was doing but unable to stop because he wanted to give someone else the hell he was having himself.

'It isn't our fault, Mr Ormond,' Miss Roper reproached him just before she left that evening.

He was off guard, worn right down by weariness and black moods. 'What isn't?' he muttered, not even looking up from the paperwork cluttering up his desk.

'Whatever is turning you into a monster. We haven't done anything. It isn't fair to shout at us because you're miserable.'

He looked up then, going dark red and eying her as if he wanted to run her over with his car.

'Miserable? What are you talking about? Who said I was miserable?'

Miss Roper shook her head at him wryly. 'If you were a woman you'd be bawling your eyes out.'

'A woman? Thank God I'm not. Women cry at the drop of a hat. I saw that blonde girl you've got out there crying when she broke one of her nails, for God's sake.'

'You'd cry if you had spent months growing your nails, buffing and manicuring them, painting them with varnish, and then one of them just breaks and you have to start all over again!'

'I wouldn't grow them in the first place, let alone paint them bright red. How can anyone work with hands ending in talons that colour?'

Miss Roper eyed him ruefully. 'Why don't you swallow that pride of yours and call the girl?'

He stiffened, eyes flashing. 'My private life is none of your business, and anyway, as it happens, I am taking Miss Wallis out tonight, so you can stop feeling sorry for me.'

'Miss Wallis?' repeated his secretary in withering tones, and he felt his face burn. 'You know I didn't mean her. She's not the woman for you, and you know it.'

'Goodnight, Miss Roper!' snarled James. She opened her mouth to say something else, and he shouted. *'Goodnight, Miss Roper!'*

She left without another word, closing the door with ultra, ultra care so that she didn't make a sound. James sat staring at the wall, his face tense, jaw aching, eyes deeply set. Was he that obvious to everyone? Was the whole office talking about him, whispering behind his back, watching him?

He tried to get back to work but his brain wouldn't operate; he was too disturbed by realising that what he had thought were his own private problems had become the subject of public discussion among his staff. Damn them.

After a few minutes he got up and walked out too. Barny was waiting to drive him home, as usual. When they got back to the house in Regent's Park James went upstairs without a word to take a shower and change, flinging off his clothes with more speed than usual, and standing for minutes under the warm jets of water with his eyes closed, wishing he had time to wallow in a bath for an hour or so. His whole body ached with exhaustion.

He was just towelling his wet hair, standing barefoot in his bedroom before getting dressed, when there was a tap on the door. 'Someone downstairs to see you, sir.'

Enid's voice made him start.

'Who is it?' Surely Fiona hadn't forgotten that he had said he would pick her up? He looked at the clock on his bedside table and saw that it was half past six; he would have had to hurry if he wanted to get dressed in time to drive to Fiona's house, so it would be a relief if she had come here instead.

'A Miss Kirby, sir,' Enid said, and James felt dizzy. His ears echoed with the sound of his blood rushing wildly around his veins. He couldn't breathe enough to speak for a second.

When he managed it his voice sounded husky, even

to him. 'I'll be down in a minute. Put her in the drawing room and offer her a drink.'

He was only wearing a white towelling robe, totally naked underneath that; he must dress before he went downstairs. Moving towards the long, fitted wardrobe on one wall he abruptly stopped, brow furrowed as his brain finally began working. Until then he had been reacting sexually, his male instincts in turmoil at the thought of her being here—now he started to think.

Why was she here? Why had she come? He would have loved to think she had come because she wanted to see him, but it couldn't be that. With any other woman he would have come to that conclusion—but not Patience. She was different. She was unlike any other woman he had ever known. No, it had to be some sort of emergency. But what? It had to be something to do with him—which meant it had to be something to do with his mother? Had she been taken ill? Patience had kept telling him how frail she was, how little time left she had. What if she...?

He drew a sharp breath, refusing to finish that thought, yet suddenly desperate to hear whatever Patience had come here to tell him. It would take too long to get dressed; he slid his bare feet into black leather slippers and hurried downstairs, almost tripping over his feet on the way in his anxiety.

He found Patience in the drawing room, a glass of white wine in her hand, standing with her back to him in front of a portrait of his father painted fifty years ago.

At the sight of her James felt his whole body jerk as if hit by a bolt of lightning.

With one long look he absorbed every detail of how she looked, as if he was made of blotting paper. It was a warm spring evening and she had put on a dark green

cotton sweater which clung to her small breasts and outlined her small waist; with it she wore a short pleated
white skirt which just skimmed her knees, leaving most
of her slender, shapely legs visible. His mouth went dry
and he swallowed. She looked wonderful.

Around her throat she wore the rose-pink scarf he had
given her; it had become entangled with the hair tumbling to her shoulders and looked like rose petals among
those tight, fiery curls.

'Hallo,' he said thickly, very aware of his body's reaction to seeing her and hoping to God she wouldn't be
given any hint of it.

She swung round and did a visible double-take, which
reminded him that he was only wearing his bathrobe.

Flushed, he gestured down at himself, muttering,
'Sorry, I only just came out of the shower—I didn't wait
to dress in case this was some sort of emergency.'

She lifted her eyes from their contemplation of his
bare legs with their faint, dark hair. Her face was gentle,
concerned. 'I'm sorry, James, I'm afraid it isn't very
good news. Your mother has had a heart attack and is
in hospital.'

'Is it serious?' He felt the blood drain from his face
and was suddenly cold, shivering.

Patience gave him a searching look, then came over
and pushed him down onto a sofa. 'You aren't going to
faint, are you?' She knelt on the sofa next to him, touching his face, her small fingers warm against his cold skin.

'No, of course not,' he said impatiently. 'Just tell me.
Is my mother going to die?'

'No, James! Don't even think that way. Really, it isn't
very serious. They said they would keep her in for a few
days, for observation and rest, but it was more of a warning; she's going to have to be more careful in future.'

She bent over him, brushing a floppy strand of dark hair back from his eyes, her fingertips soft and comforting. 'Are you okay now? You went so white. You obviously care more about her than you want anyone to know.'

He was torn in two directions. He wanted to hold her hand against his face, to lean his head forward against her and feel the warmth of her body, to take comfort from her. But he was at the same time afraid of letting her get too close; he did not want her to know too much about him. He had had a hatred of betraying too much about himself ever since he was a child. He had learnt to hide his feelings then and now it had become an obsession—the necessity for secrecy, for concealment.

'I'll be okay,' he said huskily. 'Could you pour me a brandy? I need a drink.'

She looked around vaguely. 'Where is it kept? Shall I call your housekeeper?'

'No need—it's in that cabinet over there.'

Patience was still kneeling on the sofa; now she stood up, the movement wafting the scent of her towards him. She was wearing the French perfume he had given her for her birthday. Pleasure stung inside him. His perfume, his scarf—it was as if wearing them both marked her as his own.

His heart beat painfully as he watched her walk across the room to the drinks cabinet. She moved quickly, gracefully, her short skirt swinging, and the back of her knees had a young, childlike look that made his mouth curve in tenderness. She was too young for him, he told himself, but couldn't stop watching the way her red hair glittered like fire in the light from the lamps Enid must have switched on when Patience arrived. How easy it was to imagine her living here.

Stop thinking about it. It won't happen. She has a

boyfriend her own age and probably thinks I'm almost middle-aged.

He shivered, but it wasn't simply at the thought of being middle-aged. He was in shock. It had devastated him that his mother had come so close to death; it had made him face how much it would matter to him if she died. Since she came back into his life he had rejected her, told himself he didn't care about her, she was nothing to him. It disturbed him to realise that he had been lying to himself.

Abruptly he said, 'Maybe I'd better not have that drink. I must get to the hospital and see her.'

'They won't let you, not tonight,' Patience said, turning to look at him, the cabinet door open, showing a serried rank of bottles and glasses. 'She's sedated, fast asleep. You can see her tomorrow morning.' She held up a bottle, displaying the label. 'Is this what you want?'

James nodded. 'Fine, thank you.' He paused, then asked flatly, 'When did she have the heart attack? Why didn't you let me know sooner?'

She was intent on pouring brandy into a glass—far too much; James gave a squawk.

'Hey, stop! That's a triple! If I drink as much as that I won't be able to walk straight.'

She poured some of it back into the bottle, her small hand very steady, then came over with the glass, grimacing. 'Sorry, I wasn't sure how much you drank.'

'Very little, normally.' He took the glass and swallowed some of the deep amber liquid, feeling his tongue sting and his throat turn to fire.

'I'm sorry I didn't call you at once,' Patience said, sitting down beside him on the sofa, smoothing her short skirt down over her knees while she watched his colour return. 'There wasn't time; it all happened so fast. She collapsed a couple of hours ago and we called an ambulance; luckily it arrived quickly and I went with her. They gave her some treatment in the ambulance—she was better before we got into the casualty department—but they sent her up to a specialist ward as soon as the doctor had seen her.'

'Why didn't you call me from the hospital? Did you think I wouldn't want to know? What if she had died?' Had she thought he wouldn't care? Was that what she thought of him—that he was cold and indifferent? Well, maybe he had given her good cause to think that; he had told her he couldn't forgive his mother. Nevertheless hurt jabbed at him; to cover his feelings he drank more of the brandy and coughed at the heat of it in his throat.

Patience patted his back sympathetically. 'I'm sorry, James. But I was so worried at the time that I'm afraid I had nothing else in my head; I just wanted to get her some help quickly.'

'Surely you must have had time for a quick call while she was being dealt with in Casualty?'

She didn't deny that, sighing. 'Yes, I'm sorry. I didn't think of calling you until I was leaving, and then I thought it would be better to break the news in person instead of phoning.'

'Better late than never, I suppose,' he muttered, knowing he was being ungrateful and unfair. He put the empty brandy glass down on a nearby table and looked at the clock, startled to see that it was now nearly seven.

He would be late picking Fiona up. Frowning, he stood up. 'Excuse me a second, I must make a phone call. I'm going to be late for dinner with someone.'

She gave him a quick, narrowed glance, then stood up, too. 'I'd better go, anyway.'

James was already walking across the room towards

a telephone on a small table near the fireplace. As Patience took a step towards the door they collided.

'Sorry,' she said, laughing and clutching at him to stay on her feet.

His towelling robe slipped as her fingers pulled on it, the lapels parting all the way down. James drew a shaken breath, watching her face burn as, caught unaware, she stared at his naked body only inches away from her.

'Oh…sorry…' she whispered, but kept looking at him, her hazel eyes wide and startled.

'What's the matter? Haven't you ever seen a naked man before?' he asked thickly, and her face burned.

Passion lit up inside him; he bent his head to find her mouth, catching hold of her arms to pull her closer.

Her hands tightened on his robe, her fingers curling into the soft material, and he felt his belt come undone, the white robe falling open from neck to thigh.

'I'm sorry… Ohh…' Patience gasped, her eyes wide open, staring at his body, her face hotly flushed.

Had she ever made love? Or was she a virgin? He would put money on it that she was—he couldn't believe she had ever let that boy make love to her. Taking hold of her hands, he moved them sideways until they touched his warm flesh, groaning in deep pleasure. 'Touch me.' His arms went round her, imprisoning her, propelling her even closer, capturing her hands between them, her fingers splayed wide across his chest.

She was staring up at him, her eyes enormous, her lips parted; she looked, James thought, as if she had been hypnotised.

He didn't give her time to recover. His head went down and his mouth finally caught hers, feeling her lips quivering, warm and soft and yielding. Her spread fingers were moving against his naked skin softly, like little mice looking for a way out of a trap, but at the same time she was kissing him back, and she wasn't struggling. His blood beat so fast he was almost giddy. He felt his flesh hardening, lifting; he wanted her so badly he would have died if he could just push her down onto the carpet and take her there and then.

She had to know what was happening to him; she wasn't that innocent. They were too close for her to miss the fierce pressure of his body towards her, but he didn't want to scare her or ruin this moment. He wouldn't rush anything. The last thing he wanted to do was frighten her.

She broke off the kiss suddenly, audibly drawing a long breath, as if her lungs needed air. James slid his mouth down her cheek to her neck, kissing each soft inch of her skin, his nostrils full of the scent of her. He felt her body sway backwards slightly, as if she was half fainting, and heat mounted to his head. Hungrily his mouth pushed back the neckline of her sweater and moved against her delicate collarbone, and Patience sighed.

Tentatively, half expecting her to stop him, James inserted his hands under her green sweater and found warm flesh. She was only wearing a tiny silky bra underneath the sweater; he had the fastening undone a moment later, and quickly moved his hands round to cup her escaping breasts. They were so soft and smooth, like round, warm apples.

He heard her mouth form a gasp of what he took to be shock under his kiss and froze, waiting for her to protest or get angry, but she did neither. James quickly moved his mouth back to hers. Her arms slid round his neck and she moved closer, kissing him back.

He felt the small nipples of her breasts hardening; the

flesh he was caressing grew heavier, filling his palms. She might look like a very young girl, but her body was that of a woman, and he ached to explore all of it. The very prospect made his temperature rise; he was breathing very fast, and shaking slightly.

How far was she going to let him go? His excitement spiralled, he was dizzy with it, and he pulled her even closer, pressing himself into her, one knee sliding between her legs.

Patience wrenched back her head with a loud, wordless cry, and pushed him away with a force that sent her sprawling backwards. James didn't let go of her; they fell together onto the sofa, with him landing on top. The feel of her underneath him nearly drove him crazy; he groaned, dragging her sweater upwards so that he could bury his face in the warm fullness of her breasts, his mouth searching for one of those hard pink nipples.

'Don't…no, James…I won't let you…' Her voice was shaky and barely audible; he felt her hands thrusting at him, her knees jerking upwards to push him away. 'Stop it!'

It was hard for him to drag himself out of the wild excitement; dark red and shuddering with passion he lifted his head, his eyes half-open and blinking in the sudden light as he looked down at her.

'Sorry,' he muttered thickly. 'I got carried away.'

He stumbled off the sofa, pulled his robe together, tied the belt tightly. Patience jumped up, too, moved away to a safe distance and hurriedly fumbled with her bra while he broodingly watched.

'I would have stopped any time you asked me to!' he protested, and her greeny hazel eyes slanted sideways as she pulled her sweater down and ran a hand over her tangled red hair.

'Would you? I got the feeling you weren't going to!'

Was she smiling? Even worse…laughing at him? He couldn't deny he would have gone as far as she let him; he had gone out of his head with desire for her—he still felt that terrible, burning urge. Obviously it hadn't been mutual. He had been kidding himself when he thought she wanted their lovemaking as much as he did. His overheated body cooled down as if someone had flung a bucket of icy water over it. She didn't feel the way he did at all. Why had she let him go so far?

'I wouldn't have done anything you didn't want me to do,' he said, scowling at the floor because he didn't want her to see his eyes. He was afraid his sense of hurt, of rejection might show, and that would only make his humiliation worse. 'I'm sorry, okay? I got the wrong vibes.'

'What vibes did you think you got?' She looked down, her thick ginger lashes flickering against her cheek. He saw the gleam of her hazel eyes behind them—were there tears in her eyes or was that just the lustre of her pupils?

He would give anything to know what was going on inside her head, but she was a foreign country to him; he didn't have a clue about her.

'It doesn't matter!' he said grimly.

'It does to me! What vibes did you think you were getting?'

'Never mind. Sorry. I was obviously mistaken.' He had made a fool of himself in front of the one woman in the world he did not want to think him a fool.

'About what?'

He shrugged, wordless. He wasn't admitting his own feelings when he hadn't any idea how she felt about him.

Patience asked coolly, 'Do you always try it on with every girl you meet?'

'Of course not!' Was that what she thought of him?

'Why try it on with me, then?' Her lashes lifted again, her eyes very shiny, bright with impatience or some other emotion he could not read. 'Did you think I fancied you? That I wanted you to make love to me? Why did you start making love to me? Do you fancy me, James?'

His mood was deflated, depressed; he wanted to get rid of her and try to forget what had happened in this room just now. He felt stupid. What on earth had made him imagine she would want him the way he wanted her? He had allowed himself to believe it because he wanted to!

'Why don't you say something?' she insisted. 'I didn't have you down as the sort of guy who is always making passes—so why did you make one at me?'

He resented her relentless inquisition, knowing it was down to pure female curiosity—typical of a woman to want to analyse his emotions, his thinking, everything he said. She didn't want him, but she wanted to get under his skin, make him bare his soul to her. Well, he wasn't going to!

'Sorry, I think we've said enough, and if you'll excuse me, I must get dressed,' he said with cold dignity. 'I have a date and I shall be late if I don't hurry up.'

'A date?'

'Yes, sorry. I must rush.' James turned away, walked out of the room, wanting to run to get away. He needed to be alone, where nobody could see how he felt.

Patience followed him. 'I'll show you out first,' he said without looking at her, but just as they reached the front door somebody rang the bell.

Patience opened the door before he could stop her and

they both stood staring at Fiona, who stared back at them, her arctic blue gaze sweeping from Patience's clearly dishevelled hair and rumpled sweater, her flushed face and startled eyes, to James, who was clearly naked under that white towelling robe.

Fiona's mouth tightened, her face acid. 'So that's why you were late! I was beginning to suspect you were seeing someone else.'

CHAPTER SEVEN

THERE was a silence while both women looked at James and he stared at the floor, his face rigid. He loathed scenes, especially in public, detested being shouted at by women, and hated to be made to look ridiculous—not that any of these things had ever happened to him more than once. If anyone made a scene he always put on his harshest voice to demolish them, and then vanished. If a woman shouted at him he gave her an icy look, then vanished. If he felt he had been made to look ridiculous, he vanished. He had always had a simple method of dealing with anything he did not like. He just walked away from it, fast.

Now he did not know what to do or say. Fiona was absolutely right—how could he lie to her? It was time he ended his relationship with her. He should have finished with her long ago; they were not right for each other and he should have been honest with her. She would find someone else easily enough; she was a beautiful woman, from a wealthy family—plenty of men would jump at the chance to grab her. Most of them wouldn't even care that she was cold and selfish. He had often been surprised at how many men he knew who were married to cold, selfish women without seeming to mind too much. Their wives were ornaments, not partners, presumably—or the man himself was cold and selfish, and perfectly satisfied with a wife of the same nature.

Fiona was working herself up into a tearing rage. 'If

I'd waited at home instead of driving over here to see what was holding you up I'd never have known you were playing away, would I?'

He couldn't deny that; he would probably have lied to avoid trouble.

Fiona read the admission in his face and icily elaborated. 'You'd have made up some lie about getting a vital phone call just as you were about to leave, or being caught in bad traffic—and I'd have been none the wiser, would I? How often have you lied to me in the past, I wonder? You kept telling me how busy you were at work, but I suppose you were being busy somewhere more private all the time.'

'I'm sorry, Fiona,' he said stiffly, and felt Patience looking at him, hazel eyes surprised and anxious.

She whispered, as if Fiona couldn't hear her perfectly well, 'James, don't just let it go...explain...tell her she's got the wrong idea.'

He shook his head, features rigid with pride and resentment. Why was Patience trying to push him back into Fiona's arms? He wasn't getting down on his knees, making an act of contrition, pleading with Fiona to forgive him when he wasn't sorry about anything. His whole relationship with her had been a mistake and he was relieved to get out of it.

Patience said earnestly to Fiona, 'Really, you're making a mistake. You've got it wrong. James, talk to her, make her see...'

'I have eyes,' Fiona unnecessarily informed them both. 'I can see, don't worry.' She looked them over again, distaste in her face, lingering on the rumpled state of Patience's clothes, on his bare feet and legs. 'Only too clearly. I don't need James to draw diagrams.'

Distressed, Patience said, 'No, you don't understand—it isn't what you think!'

Fiona made a noise halfway between an angry snort and a cat's sneeze. 'Will you keep out of this? I'm not talking to you. You can keep him. If you can! But take my advice—don't give up the day job. He's a lying, cheating bastard, and you needn't think he'll treat you any better than he's treated me!'

Turning on her heel, her ice-blonde head held high, she walked back to her parked red Aston Martin as if she was marching over James's face with every step, got behind the wheel, slammed the door, started the engine and drove off with a deep-throated roar, vanishing round the corner a few seconds later, so fast one almost expected flames to come out of the exhaust.

She was an excellent driver, James thought inconsequentially. A little too reckless, mind you. But only when she was in a temper. The trouble was, she flew into a temper far too often. One day she would have an accident if she wasn't careful.

Patience threw an uncertain look at him, hazel eyes questioning. 'Don't just let her go. Go after her.'

'What, in my bathrobe?' He shrugged, then said childishly, 'And, anyway, I don't run after women!'

'Don't you care about her?' Patience searched his face, her own face pale and set. 'No, obviously not. You don't really care about anyone or anything except business, do you?'

'Oh, thanks,' he said, with bitterness. So that was what she thought of him, was it? That he was cold and selfish. Oh, maybe he had been once; if he was honest he had to admit he might have been. Until he met her. She had changed his entire life. But he couldn't tell her so without betraying his feelings, giving himself away.

He wasn't going to do that. He had some pride left.

Patience said quietly, 'I'm beginning to see that your mother damaged you badly when she left you behind.' Her eyes went past him into the elegant house, came back to his face, her expression dismissive, full of rejection. 'You've got a beautiful house, James, but it's just a shell; it isn't a home. And you're the same—you're a shell, not a human being.'

His face growing even paler, he flinched from that judgement, but he wouldn't let her see she had hurt him. The old imperatives he had absorbed as a child came back—hide what you're feeling; don't let anyone guess you're unhappy or scared.

He stepped back into his house, his face white, stiff, tense with pride. 'Goodbye, Patience.' If that was what she thought of him there was no point in saying anything else—no more than there had been any point in saying anything to Fiona. Sometimes words were unnecessary, superfluous.

That evening he did not go out. While Enid was putting together a light supper for him James listened to Mozart and read a couple of that week's business magazines from the States—although his mind wasn't on anything he read, and he kept reading the same words over and over without taking in what they meant. His brain seemed to be on hold.

'I hope this is okay,' Barny told him as he brought the first course of the meal into the dining room. 'Enid didn't have much in store, thinking you would be out. She was doing the marketing tomorrow, so she had to improvise with what she had.'

'It looks fine to me,' James said indifferently, staring at the plate in front of him. Enid had halved and sliced crisp pears in a fan, topped them with fine thin strips of

pink ham, goat's cheese and walnuts, finally trickling a
delicate dressing over that. The colours were pretty, the
texture of the food interesting. He tasted some; was that
balsamic vinegar? Well, whatever it was, the flavour was
refreshing and different. A pity he had no appetite, but
to save Enid's feelings when she had gone to so much
trouble he would have to eat it—even if it choked him.

When Barny returned with the next course and looked
at his empty plate with satisfaction, James said, 'It was
delicious. Tell Enid she's a genius.'

Relief in his face, Barny grinned, whisking away the
used plate and putting down the second course. 'She
enjoys a bit of a challenge; you know that. She's tried
something new with this too—she only had the one
chicken breast, so she cut it into little goujon strips,
breadcrumbed it, and panfried it. The sauce is cream and
tarragon; she knows how much you love tarragon.'

Do I? James thought blankly, staring at the green-
flecked creamy sauce. He tasted it. Oh, yes, he liked that.
'You and Enid spoil me,' he told Barny, remembering
how often they had gone out of their way when he was
a child to get him food they knew he liked.

He refused a dessert and had his coffee served in his
study, deciding to work for a couple of hours until bed-
time. He wouldn't sleep; there was no point in going up
to bed yet.

'Is there anything else I can get you, sir?' Barny
asked, before leaving him alone there.

Looking up from the documents he was arranging in
order on his desk, James shook his head. 'No, thank you,
Barny. I'll be fine.'

Barny hesitated by the door and James looked up
again to find a look of anxiety and concern in the older
man's eyes.

'She's a very nice girl, sir,' Barny blurted out. 'Kind and warm-hearted, full of fun, but serious underneath. Not like that other one. Me and Enid, we never had time for her.'

Freezing over, James said coldly, 'Goodnight, Barny.' He wasn't discussing either Fiona or Patience; Barny had no business saying anything about either of them.

James's private life was nothing to do with anyone who worked for him; they should just do their job and mind their own business. But then that was the trouble with having staff who had known you since you were a child—like Miss Roper, they thought they could give you their opinions whenever they liked without pulling their punches. It didn't occur to them that they were taking liberties!

Barny flushed, giving him a wounded look, and withdrew without another word, leaving James feeling guilty and, at the same time, resentful. Why should he feel guilty? Rationally he knew he was right; Barny shouldn't have said anything. But after staring at the wall for some time he picked up the internal phone and rang down to the staff quarters in the basement.

Barny picked up the phone, his voice flat and polite. 'Yes, sir?'

'I'm sorry, Barny,' James said. 'I shouldn't have bitten your head off. It's just that I'm tired and irritable.'

'That's all right, sir.' Barny's voice warmed, had a hint of a smile in it. 'I understand.'

James was afraid he understood too well, and he certainly wasn't giving Barny a chance to discuss it any further, so he hurriedly said goodnight.

'Goodnight, sir.'

James put the phone down and looked at the papers in front of him. Concentrate! he ordered himself. Work was one way of forgetting everything else; he had learnt that as a boy. The words danced like midges, tiny black dots that made no sense. Pain stabbed in his head. No, not a headache now. He put a finger on the artery in his right temple, closing his eyes as the pressure eased the pain, but as soon as he stopped pushing down on the artery the pain began again, so, abandoning his work, he turned out the light and went up to bed.

He couldn't sleep, however; for a long time he tossed and turned, wide awake and yet unable to read or listen to music. All he could think about was Patience. How she felt in his arms, how soft and warm her mouth felt under his, how…

How could he bear to lose her?

Stop being such a fool! he told himself. How could you lose what you had never had?

Turning heavily, he groaned. Stop thinking about her. Get some sleep or you'll be like a corpse in the morning.

When he finally did get to sleep it was to dream about her: hot, restless dreams of holding her, naked, kissing her, entering her, of the long, intense satisfaction he needed from her, would give anything to experience.

He woke crying out, shuddering in the primrose light of dawn, and stumbled out of bed at once, shedding his damp pyjamas and dropping them into the laundry basket in his bathroom before taking a long, cool shower. Thoroughly awake by then, he dressed, avoiding meeting his own eyes in the bathroom mirror.

Nobody else was up yet; he went into his study and plugged in the electric kettle he kept there so that he could make himself instant coffee any time of the day or night, then sipped black coffee while he did some of the work he had not done the night before.

Barny appeared at seven and carefully didn't comment

on the fact that James was already up, dressed and working.

'Nice morning, isn't it?'

James had not noticed, but when Barny drew back the curtains James looked at the blue sky and sunlight blankly. Spring glittered outside but in his heart he felt like winter.

'Breakfast, sir? What would you like?'

'I'll just have some fresh orange juice. I'm not hungry and I want to finish this work before I go.'

'You ought to eat something,' Barny began, then caught James's eye and shrugged. 'All right, suit yourself. I'll get your juice.'

When he had gone James rang the hospital and was put through to the ward his mother was on, but he got very little information from the night ward sister other than that she was 'comfortable'.

'When could I come in and visit?'

'Any time between ten o'clock and twelve, or between two-thirty and four.'

When Barny brought the orange juice and some fresh coffee James told him they would be leaving for the office at eight. Without looking at Barny, he added, 'I have to visit my mother, who is in hospital.'

He heard Barny's little gasp. 'In hospital? Is it serious?' Barny sounded genuinely upset by the news.

'She had a slight heart attack, but I gather it was more of a warning than anything else. I just rang the ward and was told she was "comfortable", whatever that means. Anyway, I can't see her yet; they say I can go in later. I'll go into the office first, but then I shall want you to drive me to the hospital. While I'm at work could you go to a florist and choose some flowers for me?'

Barny nodded. 'Only too happy, sir. I'm very sorry to

hear she's ill. Me and Enid, we always liked your mother, sir. A breath of fresh air she was, while she was in this house. We were very sorry to see her go. Just a pity she didn't take you with her.'

He went before James could tell him to keep his opinions to himself. But he probably wouldn't have said that to Barny. After all, hadn't the man simply echoed his own opinion? How could he find fault with him for that?

When he went into his office later he found Miss Roper already there, going through a big pile of mail. She glanced up, as usual running an appraising eye over him, and James suddenly remembered how every morning when he'd first arrived she used to check on the clothes he was wearing, making sure he had crisp clean shirt on, a tie she approved of, well-polished shoes and a well-pressed suit.

For the first time it occurred to him that he had had two substitute mothers—Enid first, and then Miss Roper. Had he ever told either of them how grateful he was for everything they had done for him? No, of course he hadn't. Until this second he had taken it all for granted, never even noticed the care they took of him and for him.

'Good morning,' Miss Roper, said, her tone suggesting that she hoped it was going to be, anyway, unless he was in the sort of black mood he had been in yesterday.

He tried to sound cheerful. 'We're going to have to rush through anything important, Miss Roper. I have to leave again at ten. Is there anything I should know about in today's post?'

She was obviously curious about the need for haste, but didn't ask any questions—just picked up several letters she had put aside because they required instant decisions and were important. They dealt with them at once, then James sat down behind his desk and dictated several memos and letters before making some vital phone calls.

It was nearly ten when he ended the last call; he looked at his watch, sighing.

'I don't know when I'll be back.'

'You have a lunch appointment with the chairman of Hortley Enterprises—shall I try to cancel it?'

'Maybe you should—where were we meeting?'

'Your club.'

He nodded. 'Oh, yes, I remember now. He's a member, too. Give his secretary a ring and apologise. Say I'll be in touch very soon to suggest a new date.'

She made a note on her pad. 'Yes, sir. What about the afternoon appointments?' She read them out and he hesitated.

'I'm not sure—I may be able to keep them. I'll ring if I can't make it. And if you need me urgently ring Barny on the car phone and he'll get a message to me.' He had not been going to tell her about his mother, but suddenly decided to do so. 'My mother has had a slight heart attack and is in hospital. I have to visit her and I don't know what I'll find, so I can't be sure how long I shall be there.'

Her face changed; she looked at him with distressed sympathy. 'Oh, I am sorry—was it a bad attack?'

'Fortunately not, I gather, but I haven't seen her yet. It only happened last night.'

'Well, give her my best wishes for a speedy recovery.'

He nodded, smiled at her. 'I will. Thank you, Miss Roper.'

He saw surprise in her eyes and flushed a little—wasn't he always polite to her? Well, maybe not, honesty forced him to admit. If you wanted to be successful in business these days you had to be ruthless, and that required a focusing of your energy, a tension and hardness that spilled out into everyday relationships with staff around you. Perhaps he had let that ruthlessness become a hard shell which kept his staff at a distance? He had never meant to let that happen. He must do something about it.

As he left he almost collided with the little blonde girl, who gave a squeak of horror at the sight of him and began babbling excuses.

'I'm sorry I'm late. I overslept, missed my train...'

'Don't tell me, tell Miss Roper. She runs the office, not me,' James said, striding past, but giving her a smile which made her look even more terrified, her big eyes opening even wider, her mouth a round O.

Barny was waiting as ordered, a huge bouquet of spring flowers on the back seat of the car: long-stemmed golden daffodils, pink and white tulips, purple and white and yellow freesias. The colour and scent of them was overwhelming in the car interior. If he hadn't been so depressed they would have made him feel good to be alive. They didn't.

'I hope they're what you had in mind,' said Barny anxiously, watching his face.

Forcing a smile, he nodded. 'Magnificent, thank you, Barny. I'm sure she'll love them. I don't know how long I'll be in the hospital, so I suggest you go home when you've dropped me off. I'll get a taxi there when I leave.'

Traffic was heavy; it took them longer to reach the hospital than James had expected. It was half past ten before Barny dropped him off in front of the main entrance, came round and opened the door for him.

'Would you give our best wishes to Madam? From me and Enid. We hope she'll be better soon and we look forward to seeing her again before too long.'

James nodded. 'Yes, I'll tell her.' He had picked up what Barny had not actually said—that they were expecting that he would soon bring his mother home to live with him. When he'd first seen her again he would have sworn such a possibility would never arise. How rapidly things changed; how soon you got accustomed to ideas you would have sworn at first that you would never entertain.

Oh, he still didn't know if he could forgive her, put the past behind him enough to bring her home to live with him. Certainly not yet. He was not going to leap before he looked; he was too wary a bird to make a hasty move. In any case, if she left Patience's home he would never see Patience again. He flushed at that admission, faintly ashamed. Was he really putting his own needs before his mother's happiness?

Once upon a time he would have reminded himself that that was what his mother had done to him when he was a child. He would have thought: She deserves what she has got.

This heart attack had changed everything overnight. He felt very differently this morning. He was going to have to make plans for his mother urgently now. Of course, she might wish to stay with Patience—after all, she had all that company there. The house was full of people of her own age, not to mention the three children and all their pets. Who would not rather stay there than come to live in his empty, silent house? But he must give her the choice, invite her to come home with him.

He arrived at his mother's bedside to find her fast asleep, her hands outside on the woven white bedcover, her body linked up to several pieces of equipment that gave her an extra-terrestrial look.

The ward sister let him stand by her bed for a short time, took his flowers and put them into several vases, then beckoned from the door, her finger to her lips. James obediently tiptoed out, wincing as his leather soles squeaked on the highly polished floor, in case he woke his mother.

'You can wait outside in the corridor, if you wish. She may wake up in a little while. She tends to take cat naps with waking gaps in between, which is good. She's comfortable, but what she needs is lots of rest. I'll call you if she wakes, or you can come back this afternoon.'

'Is she going to be okay?' he asked huskily. 'I mean...how serious was the attack?'

'Obviously it was serious enough for hospitalisation, which means that she'll have to make some changes in her lifestyle, which her specialist will explain to her.'

'Can I see him?'

'He isn't here this morning. You could see him after his round, at five o'clock. Can you come back?'

'Five? Yes, I'll come back then. If I'm needed, here are my phone numbers.' He wrote them on a piece of paper and handed them to the sister, but instead of leaving the hospital sat down outside on a chair in the corridor for a while.

He was so cold, shivering slightly, that it dawned on him that he must be in shock after seeing his mother lying in that white bed, small and pale and childlike. She looked so old and ill. Was she going to die, despite what that ward sister had said?

He felt so odd that he knew he could not sit through his business meetings, so he rang his office on his mobile and told Miss Roper to cancel his afternoon appointments.

'Yes, sir, I'll do that right away,' she said, then asked, 'How was your mother?'

'She's sedated; I didn't get a chance to talk to her. The sister said she was going to be okay, but—' He broke off, swallowing.

'But what?' prompted Miss Roper, and he sighed.

'But I thought she looked terrible. Expect me when you see me, Miss Roper.'

He rang off, feeling really strange, dizzy and light-headed. He was afraid he might faint so he leaned right down, his head between his knees, waiting for the faintness to pass.

'James? What's wrong? She isn't...?' Patience's voice was rough with urgency and worry.

He sat up too quickly; his head went round and round as if he was in a washing machine.

She dazzled his eyes, hair blazing above a very pale face, greeny hazel eyes enormous and dark with dilated pupils. He blinked at her, his heart crashing against his ribs with a rushing sound, like the sea on rocks.

'James? What is it? Tell me,' she thickly insisted.

He realised what she was afraid he might say, quickly shook his head. 'No, no, she isn't dead,' he hurried to reassure her. 'She's asleep. I'm waiting in case she wakes up.'

She gave a long sigh of relief and sat down abruptly on the chair next to him. 'Thank God for that. When I saw you looking so stressed I thought... But why did you have your head down like that, then?'

He grimaced. 'I was feeling a little weird.' She searched his face and he hurriedly said, 'I'm okay now.'

She looked like spring in a lime-green tunic-style

dress under a darker green jacket. He felt his spirits lifting at the sight of her. Huskily he said, 'The ward sister seems to think she's doing well. Well, ''comfortable'', she said, but then that's what they always say, isn't it? Meant to reassure you, but does it mean much?'

'They wouldn't lie, James—if they say she's comfortable I think they mean it. Otherwise they would be in trouble if she died, wouldn't they?'

'I suppose so.' His eyes roved down over her slender legs to her small feet in white sandals. Was she dressed up to meet that boyfriend of hers for lunch after visiting his mother?

'What are you staring at?'

He curtly said, 'I didn't know I was.'

'Well, you were. Don't you like my dress? Or was it my shoes you were making faces over?'

'Of course not. I wasn't making faces. It wasn't that...I mean, I was doing nothing of the kind.' He knew he sounded confused; he was gibbering like a fool. She had that effect on him. He had always prided himself on his self-control. Where was it now? What on earth must she be thinking? He had to pull himself together.

The ward sister came out and looked at them both. 'I thought you'd gone,' she told James. 'There's really no point in waiting. Why don't you come back this afternoon?'

Patience stood up. 'How is she?' she asked the other woman, who smiled at her in a friendly way.

'Oh, hello again. You came with her when she was brought in, didn't you? I remember you. She's much better today; I don't suppose we'll have her with us much longer—just a few days.'

'That's wonderful. Well, I'll come back and see her later, then.'

They walked out of the hospital together. James was grimly silent. He couldn't think of anything to say to her. Outside the building Patience glanced up at him.

'Did your chauffeur bring you? Is he waiting?'

'No, I was going to take a taxi back.'

'I've got my car; I'll give you a lift.'

'I didn't know you had a car.'

'I couldn't manage without one, especially for the shopping. To save money I buy in bulk, which means a lot of shopping at one time.'

She turned to the right and walked through the hospital car park with James at her heels, stopping beside a large red, old, very battered four-wheel drive estate car. Unlocking the driver's door, she gestured. 'Hop in. Where are you going? Your office?'

He got into the passenger seat, looked at his watch and was startled to see that it was now nearly twelve. 'Have you got a lunch date?'

She slid in beside him, behind the wheel. 'Only with a shopping trolley on the way home.'

His heart skipped. So she wasn't meeting that boy! 'Let me buy you lunch,' he said offhandedly.

Her voice was teasing. 'There's no need to offer me lunch, James, just because I give you a lift!'

She was infuriating; why couldn't she accept the invitation without arguing? He scowled at her. 'I'm inviting you because I want to.'

She looked down, her lashes golden in the sunlight, her eyes gleaming behind them like shimmering water between reeds.

'Then I'd love to—where shall we go?'

'I'll book somewhere.' He pulled his small mobile phone out of his inner pocket and dialled rapidly.

Barny answered within seconds. 'Hallo? This is the Ormond residence.'

'Hallo, Barny. Can Enid do lunch for two?'

'Of course. Is Madam coming home? Is she better?'

'She is better, but she still has to stay in hospital.' He paused, added tersely, 'Lunch isn't for her. We'll be there in about twenty minutes.'

'Anything in particular you wanted Enid to do? She stocked the fridges and larders this morning; she could do anything you liked.'

'Something special,' he said, and rang off.

Patience had started the engine. Without looking at him she said, 'Do I gather we're lunching at your house?'

'If that's okay.'

Her lashes flicked briefly to him, then away. 'So long as it's just lunch you're offering.'

She backed the car out of the space it occupied, turned to the left and began driving out of the car park while James dwelt on her last remark, his face darkening.

'What's that supposed to mean?'

Turning out onto the road, she slid into heavy traffic with a skill he noticed with some surprise. She was a good driver, far more careful than Fiona, although she was so much younger and must be far less experienced.

'Oh, come on, James,' she murmured without looking at him. 'Do you think I've forgotten what happened at your house yesterday, before your girlfriend turned up? Lunch, yes. Sex, no. Okay?'

'I got your message loud and clear yesterday,' he muttered, glowering ahead at the thick traffic, his face hardening, red stains across his cheekbones. 'You'll be perfectly safe, don't worry. I won't make a pass again.'

He wished to God he hadn't invited her to lunch—he

must be out of his mind. She had made it plain that she did not like him, let alone fancy him. Being alone with her, knowing she felt like that, would be painful, frustrating, humiliating.

Bitterness welled up inside him. Why had this happened to him? What had he ever done to deserve it? He had had such a bleak childhood, without any sign of affection from his father, which was why it had taken him all his adult life to fall in love for the first time. He hadn't wanted to risk getting hurt, which made what was happening to him now so ironic. When he did fall he had fallen hard for the wrong woman. She couldn't stand him, but he was crazy about her, obsessed, couldn't get her out of his head day and night.

It was all some sort of black joke.

CHAPTER EIGHT

JAMES was silent as Patience drove towards Regent's Park. Head averted, he stared bleakly out of the half-open window, his black hair blowing back in a light spring breeze, looking at the crowded streets but not really seeing any of the people hurrying along, the shops and office blocks, or the cars, taxis, lorries moving slowly beside Patience's vehicle. He was too conscious of her beside him, her small hands moving firmly and confidently on the wheel. For days now she had occupied the centre of his mind, a clear, sharp image dominating his thoughts while everything else in the whole wide world seemed to fade away like shadows in twilight. What on earth had he thought about before me met her? How had he spent his days? He found it difficult to remember, but he knew that nothing in his life had had much meaning.

'Don't sulk!' she said suddenly, and he started violently, turning then to give her a cold, affronted stare.

'I was doing nothing of the kind!' Did she have to talk to him as if he were a child? Women could be so condescending; there was a smug centre to thcm, perhaps because they were the ones who had the babies, brought up the children, ran the home. They were always sure they were right about everything.

'Oh, yes, you were—you've been sitting there for the past ten minutes with a scowl on your face, throbbing with rage. If you're going to be in that sort of mood we're going to have a very uncomfortable lunch.'

His dreamy mood of a few minutes ago evaporated. He wasn't telling her how wrong she was—he couldn't tell her how he really felt—so he furiously counter-attacked.

'Trying to get out of having lunch with me now, are you? Typical of a woman. You want an excuse for changing your mind about lunch so you try to claim it's all my fault you won't come.'

They drew up at traffic lights in Swiss Cottage. Her small hands resting on the wheel, Patience turned her head to eye him, the tangle of windblown red curls blowing across her face.

'I'm not the one in a foul temper.'

'If I'm angry it's because you accused me of inviting you to lunch just to get you into bed.'

'After last night what do you expect? After all, I was only there to tell you your mother was very ill—the last thing I expected was to have you jump me. I should have remembered that all men ever have on their minds is sex.'

He was too angry to trust himself to reply, so he turned his head away, grinding his teeth, only to find himself facing the fascinated eyes of a blonde girl in a sleek blue sports car which was idling beside them wait-ing for the lights to change. She had obviously overheard what he and Patience were saying. As their eyes met, she winked, grinning.

James gave her an affronted look, turning his head back towards Patience, who was resting her forearms on the wheel, her head forward. She had seen his exchange of glances with the blonde in the blue car, seen the other girl wink at him. James couldn't believe his eyes when he saw Patience grin and wink back.

Women! he thought bitterly. Sisters under the skin,

wasn't that what people always said? What they meant
was that women loved to conspire together, laugh secretly at men, share jokes against them. No wonder they
were often called the opposite sex—women were always
opposing men, at first secretly, in the far away time when
men ran the world, but now that feminism had changed
the way the world worked women were in open con-
frontation with the men around them. It was war, not
love they wanted to make.

The lights changed and they drove off. 'So what did
we decide?' Patience asked him.

He started, lost in his own black thoughts. 'What
about?'

'To lunch or not to lunch? Are you still brooding over
what I said, or are you going to be grown-up enough to
make the effort to be nice if I come to your home?'

'I am always polite to guests in my home,' he said
stiffly. Even guests who shared jokes against him with
other women.

'*Nice*, I said, not polite. I know how chilly you can
be! Putting up with you in that mood would take away
my appetite.'

They were in Regent's Park by then, driving round
the circular maze of streets surrounding the park. Today
there were plenty of people about: enjoying the sunshine
and spring weather on the green lawns, walking by the
canal to feed bread to the dozens of ducks and other
water birds, or moving towards London's famous zoo,
children running and skipping ahead of their parents,
lovers holding hands under the trees or lying together
kissing on the grass.

During the winter months the park paths were empty
except for people taking a short cut to work or taking a
dog for a walk. Lovers preferred to do their kissing in-

doors in cold weather, but Londoners returned, like the swallows, to the parks as soon as spring began. James stared at one pair with a mixture of envy and resentment. You could see from the way they were stroking each other's faces while gazing into each other's eyes that this young couple were passionately in love. He could never remember lying on the park grass like that. His education and background made him far too self-conscious.

He thought of walking hand-in-hand with Patience under those weeping willows, stopping in the green tent of branches, hidden from prying eyes, to kiss her, touch her. Frustration ate at him. It would never happen, however much he ached for it.

'Are you even listening?' Patience demanded.

Eyes flashing, he turned back to her. 'Of course I am. I don't have much choice, do I, when you keep nagging at me? Anyone would think we were married! What do you want me to do—beg you to have lunch with me? Because you're out of luck. I am not going on my knees to you or any other woman.'

The roughness of his voice was bred by a feverish desire to kiss her, to stroke her cheek, let her red hair trickle through his fingers, but she wasn't to know that.

She drew up outside his home and glared back at him. 'You see? We haven't even started eating lunch and we're yelling at each other. I'd better not come in. Apologise to your housekeeper for me. I hope she didn't go to too much trouble.'

Desperation had him by the throat. He didn't want her to go. How was he ever to get to know her better if they were never alone? Her own house was so busy and crowded. But he wasn't making a fool of himself to get her to stay. His sense of his own dignity and self-respect wouldn't let him. Think! he told himself. What can I say to make her change her mind? His brain was full of fog. He forced himself to concentrate, and an idea suddenly popped up.

Hoping he sounded cool and indifferent, he shrugged and said offhandedly, 'If you insist. I don't intend to argue—go if that's what you want—but I did hope to have a serious talk to you about my mother's future. I thought you were concerned enough to want to discuss what should happen to her now, but of course if I was wrong about that then forget it.'

Her hazel eyes stared into his cold grey ones, hunting for clues about his real intentions, no doubt. He gazed back, hoping she could read nothing he would not want her to glimpse. She might be years younger than him but she was oddly adult in the way her mind worked, in how she reacted in difficult situations.

Patience had had to grow up fast when her parents died and she'd been left with the responsibility for her brothers and little sister. You couldn't help admiring the way she had coped, her ingenuity in opening a boarding-house so that they could all stay in their home, her hard work and warmth in dealing with the old people she took in as guests. It couldn't have been easy, any of it.

Many girls her age would have yearned to have fun, go out every night with boys, have new clothes, go to parties while they were young enough to enjoy that life. Few would be prepared to dedicate themselves to a lot of housework, cooking, old people, children and animals. Patience had so little time to herself. Didn't she ever feel like rebelling? He had never seen any signs of rebellion in her eyes.

'Of course I'm concerned about her!' she said, frowning.

'Good. Then come in, have lunch, and we'll talk.'

James opened the door before she could change her mind, climbed down out of the high four-wheeled drive, closed the door again and walked round to her side of the vehicle to help her down. But she had already jumped to the road and was locking her door when he got there.

She halted on the drive to look at his garden. 'Aren't they lovely?' she said, admiring the sprays of pink almond blossom on the bare black boughs of the almond trees fringing the lawn. 'And you have a wonderful display of spring flowers—just look at those flowerbeds full of daffodils and hyacinths. Our garden is never this immaculate—you can't have a perfect garden if you have children and dogs, not to mention a whole flock of bantams.'

'You know you'd rather have the children and dogs, and I imagine you get lots of eggs from the hens,' James drily said, and she laughed, a little dimple appearing at the side of her generous mouth.

'Well, of course, but it would be great to have a garden this beautiful as well!'

'And I would rather have your garden. I never had a secret den like Tom and Emmy do; I envy theirs.'

'I had a den when I was their age. I remember spending hours in it and getting told off for coming in covered in mud and grass stains.'

Barny had opened the door, stood there watching them, his face indulgent and relaxed. Patience turned to smile, walking towards him. 'Hallo, Barny, how are you?'

He beamed. 'Very well, miss, thank you. You're looking well. I hope you found Madam better this morning.'

'She is still sedated—we'll have to wait to see her

later today—but they don't seem to think it's too serious, thank heavens.'

'That's good news. Let me take your jacket.' Barny helped her shed it and took it over his arm carefully. 'Lunch will be ten minutes, sir. Shall I serve drinks first?'

'I'll pour them myself.' James was faintly irritated—listening to Patience and Barny, he had got the distinct impression that he was the target of a conspiracy. The way they talked about his mother made it plain that they had both decided she would be coming here to live before long. Whose life was it? His or theirs?

He ushered Patience into the drawing room, gesturing to an armchair. 'What can I get you to drink?'

'Just mineral water, thanks.'

He wasn't surprised, and didn't try to persuade her to drink anything else; he had the idea that she did not drink very much at all. At her home he had noticed that she only sipped a little of the rough red wine that had been passed around. Patience had a stronger will than any woman he had ever met, including Fiona. She might be young, but she was gently formidable without being icy, the way Fiona could be.

'Sparkling water?'

She nodded, and he opened a bottle of sparkling mineral water, poured some into a tall glass, then paused, ice tongs in hand, to look enquiringly at her.

'Ice?'

'No, thanks, it makes it flat. But I'll have a slice of that lemon.'

He cut a slice and dropped it into the water, poured himself a glass of gin and tonic, added ice, and walked over to give Patience her drink before sitting down facing her in another chair, nursing his glass.

Her gaze was wandering around the room until it fastened on the portrait of his father. He had still been young when the picture was painted, but somehow he looked old already. The artist had set him against the background of his office, sitting behind his leather-topped desk, at which James now sat every day, wearing City clothes—grey suit, grey silk tie, crisp white shirt. A window behind him showed grey city roofs and a grey morning sky. The impression left was entirely wintry, stiff and formal, forbidding.

Patience transferred her stare to James, frowning. 'Was he always as chilly as he looks?'

'Always.'

She nodded, still staring, her forehead corrugated. 'You do look very like him.'

'Physically,' he agreed in a flat, toneless voice.

He had been afraid that he might be turning into his father, but now he was sure he never would. He might have done if he hadn't met Patience just at the right moment. That had been the watershed of his life. He knew he would look back on that meeting as changing everything. Since meeting her he had changed beyond recognition; he might look the same on the surface, but now at the depths of his personality life was stirring, tiny roots growing upwards from the cold, frozen dark towards the light and warmth. She had come into his life like rain, breeding new life.

What would happen to him if she went out of his life again? He couldn't bear to think about it.

Swallowing hard, he said roughly, 'When my mother comes out of hospital what's going to happen to her? Is she going to need nursing at home? That would be a lot of work for you. Of course she could come here, and I could hire a nurse to take care of her, but is that what she would really want?'

Patience gave him a sarcastic smile. 'You know perfectly well she wants to be with you!'

'Are you so sure about that? Think about it. If she comes here she will be alone all day while I'm at work, and I also have quite a busy social life. I go out to dinner several evenings a week, both with friends and clients, and I get invited to parties at weekends. And I have to go away quite a bit on business. She wouldn't see much of me, you know.'

Frowning, Patience slowly said, 'No, of course not. But she would be in her own home and...'

'Don't you think she'll miss Lavinia and Joe and the others? From what I've seen I believe my mother is very happy with you and them, not to mention the children, the whole atmosphere of family life.' He drank some of his gin, his brows together as he looked up at the portrait of his father on the wall. 'She was never happy in this house. I wouldn't want to shut her up in it again unless that's really what she wants.'

Patience worried her lower lip with her small white teeth. 'That hadn't occurred to me. You may be right. She does love the company at my house, and she gets on well with Lavinia and loves the children. Well, the answer is obvious. Ask her. She's the only one who knows what she really wants.'

He nodded. 'When? Shall I wait for her to be discharged, or ask her today?'

'I think it would be best to wait until we're sure she's over this heart attack, don't you?'

'The last thing I want to do is upset her,' he agreed, just as Barny came in to tell them lunch was served.

Patience looked curiously around the large dining

room, with its mahogany woodwork and furniture, deep-piled carpet and heavy red velvet curtains. The table was laid with silver and crystal, their surfaces picked up and reflected by the chandelier overhead. There was a low, small circular glass bowl of spring flowers in the centre of the table and Barny had laid their places opposite each other so that they could talk easily across the table.

He served the first course immediately—a cold starter: pale greeny-yellow sliced melon, interleaved with sliced avocado in a fan shape, sprinkled with small prawns and strawberries. They both enjoyed the refreshing coolness of the fruit, the mixture of textures.

Enid had risen to the occasion in spectacular fashion, following that with a cheese and spinach soufflé, served with a green salad of rocket, raw young spinach and cucumber. Barny brought up a chocolate mousse for pudding and Patience groaned with pleasure as she ate a small helping.

'I dare not eat any more, but it's a dream,' she told Barny. 'Light as air. I had to eat it to stop it floating off my plate.'

'Tell Enid it was a triumph,' James agreed. 'She's a marvel, coming up with a meal like that at such short notice.'

'Well, she had the mousse made, but everything else was impromptu,' Barny said, looking delighted.

'I've never eaten food that good. I'd like to come and shake her hand in a minute,' Patience said.

'I'm sure she would be delighted to meet you, miss.' He had brought a tray of coffee with him and gestured to it. 'Shall I serve the coffee now? Will you take it here or in the drawing room?'

'In the drawing room,' James decided, leading the

way, knowing Barny would prefer that as it would give him time to clear the dining room table.

Barny carried the silver tray into the room, set it down on a low coffee table, poured them each a small cup, offered sugar and cream, and left.

Patience glanced around the room, frowning as if something in it annoyed her.

'What now?' James asked impatiently, his brows pulling together.

She turned her wide hazel eyes on to him, face innocent. 'What?'

'I saw that expression and I'm beginning to recognise it. What don't you like about this room?'

'I wasn't thinking about this room—I was thinking about the dining room.'

'What about it?'

'Victorian,' she said firmly. 'Just like something out of a film of some Victorian novel—heavy dark wood and all that red velvet. I'd find it suffocating if I had to live with it.'

'What sort of house would you like to live in?'

'I like my own home best.'

He stared down into his half-finished cup of coffee. 'One day you'll get married, though, and have to move out.'

'Not for years and years. I promised the children that we would never leave our home until they were all grown up. I can't break my promise.'

'So if you get married...'

'My husband would have to move in with us.'

She reached for the coffee pot to pour herself another cup. James quickly anticipated her, lifting the heavy, ornate silver pot to pour the coffee for her.

As he handed her cup to her their fingertips brushed. He drew a sharp breath of reaction and their eyes met.

Her pink mouth quivered, distinctly quivered. James felt his heartbeat crash violently. What did that look mean? His mind was in chaos; he was engulfed in feeling.

At that second a car drew up outside the house, the engine cut out and then they both heard the car door open and close, heard the gate pushed open, then the sound of footsteps on the long drive. The front doorbell rang sharply.

'Who on earth can that be, calling here during the lunch hour?' James turned his head to listen as Barny quietly walked through the hall. The front door was opened, then a clipped voice made James sit up, stiffening.

Oh, no, not Fiona again! What was she doing here?

Patience looked distinctly uneasy, too. Had she recognised Fiona's icy accents?

They heard Barny protesting, then the tip-tap of high heels through the hall. The drawing room door was flung open with a crash. James had been expecting it by then, yet it still made him jump like a startled hare, turning to stare and meeting Fiona's freezing gaze which moved from him to Patience.

'So she's here again! Or didn't she ever leave? Has she been here all night?'

Patience went pink, breathlessly said, 'Look, I tried to explain last night—I've been looking after his mother—that's why I was here, to tell him she had had a heart attack.'

'His mother is dead!'

'No, she isn't, but she is very ill. We've just been visiting her in hospital and James wanted to talk about future arrangements for her; that's why he invited me to lunch.'

For a moment Fiona considered that reply, staring at the coffee tray with its used cups. 'Are you a nurse?' Her tone was offhand, insulting. Patience was not looking very happy, but she answered politely.

'No, I run a boarding-house for old people, which is where Mrs Ormond has been living. That's how I met James...Mr Ormond.'

'I don't understand any of this, James,' Fiona said, transferring her attention to him. 'You have never mentioned your mother. I'm almost certain you told me she was dead.'

He shrugged, impatient at having to discuss his mother with her.

'I hadn't seen or heard of her for years; she was more or less dead to me. My parents were divorced when I was small. I never thought I'd ever hear from my mother again; it was quite a shock when she turned up again recently.' He impatiently added, 'Fiona, what are you doing here?'

'My father rang your office this morning to talk to you, and was told you weren't at work because your mother had had a heart attack. Of course we were taken aback because we'd always thought she was already dead. Frankly, we decided it must be a pretty lame and pathetic excuse for not talking to us. So I came round to ask you what exactly was going on. Why on earth didn't you tell me all this last night?'

'I had other things on my mind,' he curtly said.

Her blue eyes hunted across his face, looking for clues to what he was thinking, feeling. 'I'd have thought you would want to explain the situation to me—or didn't you care what I thought?'

'Of course he did!' Patience intervened. 'Don't you know that's just how he is? He can't talk about his feelings. That ghastly father of his trained him to be very formal, stiff upper lip and all that. It's impossible for him to admit he has any emotions. He's scared stiff of showing them.' She got to her feet. 'While I'm here he won't open up, so I'll go and talk to Barny and Enid. I wanted to get to know them anyway, and you can have James to yourself.'

James got to his feet hurriedly but she had already whisked out of the room, closing the door behind her. Well, that was that. What other proof did he need? She wouldn't leave him alone with Fiona if she cared twopence about him. He certainly wouldn't leave her alone with another man, even with that boy who was always hanging around her. Love was jealous, possessive, fierce. She didn't love him. His heart's blood ran cold.

'She seems to think she knows you rather better than I do,' Fiona glacially observed. 'How long have you known her?'

James gave her a blank look, then realised what she had asked. 'She told you—just a little while, since I found out that my mother was boarding with her.'

'Months?'

'Days,' he said, with conscious irony because it felt like years. He had been through so much since the day he first met Patience.

Fiona's brows rose again, pencilled black on her smooth, cool skin. 'I've known you for years, but obviously there's a key to you that I never discovered but this girl has.'

Their eyes met. James didn't know what to say to her. He knew what he wanted to say: Please, go away, Fiona. Just go away and forget you ever met me. But how could he say that politely? Human relationships were so complex, so tangled, words couldn't adequately deal with them.

Perhaps his eyes were more eloquent than he was, because Fiona's lips compressed, a glitter of anger in her blue eyes, then she opened her mouth and said bluntly, 'It's over, isn't it? Whatever that girl says, the truth is it's all over between us.'

He took a deep breath and went for the hard hammer of truth; there was no point in trying to tell her gently—that would only confuse the issue even further. He had to say it how it was now, and end it for good.

'Yes, you're right, it's over. I'm sorry Fiona, I made a mistake. I think we both did. I'm sorry if I misled you, but if you're honest, Fiona, your heart was never involved any more than mine was. We had fun together and we had a lot in common. We might have had a successful partnership, but never a good marriage. I didn't love you and you didn't love me. How could we have been happy together?'

'Don't go all romantic on me, James! What I always liked about you was your cool common sense. I never thought I'd hear you babbling on about hearts and flowers!'

'Falling in love changes how you see everything, Fiona. I'm not the man you thought you knew. I don't think I even know myself any more.'

'What are you talking about? You aren't making any sense.'

'On the contrary, I'm making more sense than ever before in my entire life.'

'Do you really think you'll be happy with that very boring, ordinary little girl?'

His jaw clenched; anger burnt in his eyes. 'Leave Patience out of this.'

Her mouth twisted cynically. Suddenly she looked ugly; that beauty of hers was skin-deep—peel that off and what was underneath was far from lovely.

'Oh, come off it. Don't lie to me. Do you think I haven't seen the way you look at her?'

He was appalled. Was he that obvious?

Fiona's tone changed, became ultra-sweet, saccharine. 'James, have some sense! She's not in your league. She's too young, for a start; she's unsophisticated, naive, she doesn't know how to dress, how to behave. Oh, she's pretty in a brash, loud way, no doubt she's got lots of energy and bounce, but your friends would all be horrified, would laugh at you. Men of your age often get infatuated with common little girls. It's just a temporary madness. You'll get over it, without too much damage being done, unless you make the insane mistake of marrying her! Can't you see how wrong she would be for you? She wouldn't have a clue how to talk to your friends, or how to run your home. You'd be bored stiff in weeks and then it would cost you an arm and a leg to get rid of her.'

Suddenly so angry he felt his head might explode, James snapped, 'That may be what you think, but you could be underestimating her! Maybe she has a lot more to offer than you think.'

'Sex, you mean?' Fiona's lashes drooped; she looked at him through them in a measuring, calculating way. 'Are you already sleeping with her? Maybe it's better to get it out of your system, sate yourself with her, then you'll see she would never fit in with your lifestyle.'

James snapped, 'As you just said, Patience is unsophisticated and innocent, and, no, I'm not sleeping with her. She isn't the type to sleep around—but even if I was it would be none of your business.' He turned away to walk to the door and she caught his arm, talking rapidly, breathlessly, her face burning.

'I know I said I'd rather wait to go to bed until we were married, but I'm not frigid, James, if that's what you think. I just wanted to make it special when it did happen. And it could be, James; it could be wonderful.'

He was deeply embarrassed. 'Please, this is getting us nowhere, Fiona.'

She didn't seem to hear him. She was too determined to say whatever she had come here to say. 'Whatever this girl does for you in bed I could do better, because you and I are the same sort of people, from the same sort of world. We have much more in common.'

Looking down at her, he wondered how he had ever persuaded himself that he and Fiona had anything in common. On the surface, okay, but not deep down. She was not only cold, she had a cheap, coarse-grained mind. She knew the price of everything and the real value of nothing.

Moving closer, she put her arms around his neck, her body pushing against his. James froze, not liking to push her away but not wanting her to touch him or kiss him. Skin dark red, his eyes unable to meet hers, he struggled to think of some polite way of ending this ghastly scene without offending her for ever.

'No, Fiona, please. Don't do this!' he muttered, reaching for her shoulders to move her backwards. But a second later her mouth was on his and she was kissing him in a way she never had before, her lips apart, her tongue probing his mouth with an icy sensuality which sent a shiver down his spine.

He stood there, rigid with shock and dismay, not responding. There was something chilling in the kiss, something mechanical, false. Fiona was silently offering herself, but James knew that if she wanted him it was for his money, not his body.

Behind them the door opened quietly and James stiffened, pulling his head back and trying to look round, but as he did so Fiona reached up with both hands to clasp his head and drag it back down towards her coaxing mouth. The door closed again a second later.

It had been Patience. He knew it, his heart twisting inside him. What must she be thinking? But he knew. She had seen him in Fiona's arms; she would have leapt to immediate conclusions. He had to tell her she was wrong, she was mistaken, what she had seen didn't mean a thing. Desperately he thrust Fiona away, without caring now if he annoyed or upset her, and ran to the door to open it just in time to see the front door closing. By the time he got out onto the drive Patience was driving away and she didn't look back.

CHAPTER NINE

BARNY drove him to the hospital half an hour later. Fiona had gone without saying a word to him, stalked past him with head averted, every inch of her tense with rage—and this time he knew it really was the end. All over; finally and forever. For him, of course, it had been from the day he'd set eyes on Patience, although it had taken him a little while to realise what had happened to him. He realised he had always known he didn't love Fiona—but meeting Patience had shown him that marriage without love would be an icy hell.

Fiona was a clever woman; she had quickly become aware of a change in him, he was certain of that, which made it all the more baffling that she had tried so hard to get him back, when he knew without a shred of uncertainty that she wasn't in love with him, either. So why had she persisted? Why the insistent attempt to seduce him?

That had been totally out of character. She had never acted that way before. Fiona was cool and collected, even calculating; she wasn't highly sexed or sensual, and never, never emotional. There must be something powerful driving her, though. It had nothing to do with him, or how she felt about him, so what was it? Even while she was kissing him he had been aware that it was all deliberate, planned, a cold campaign; neither her heart nor her body was truly involved. Whatever the motive, it had to be important to her. Fiona would never have put so much energy into anything important to someone else. Her life was built on the rock of her own self-interest. Nothing else mattered to her.

If only she hadn't turned up while Patience was here! If only Patience hadn't witnessed that little scene in the drawing room! Had it mattered to her? Had she cared? Why had she vanished like that?

James had stood on the drive pulsating with anxiety, anger, frustration, wishing to God he understood what went on inside women's heads. He had to talk to Patience as soon as possible. She must be going back to the hospital—he would catch up with her there and make her listen, make her see that Fiona meant nothing to him. He had turned to rush back into the house to ask Barny to drive him to the hospital at once.

That had been when Fiona appeared in the doorway. While he'd been running after Patience she had taken the time to put herself back together again after he had so roughly pushed her away. Her make-up and hair were immaculate once more. You would never suspect for an instant that she was not totally in command. Her eyes were as freezingly arctic as ever, her head held high, an icy contempt in her expression.

Sweeping past him without pausing, although James felt the rage, the hatred, radiating in his direction, she had walked to her red Aston Martin, got behind the wheel, slammed the door shut and had driven off with a tigerish roar, vanishing round the corner a moment later.

Barny had stood in the doorway. 'She's gone, then,' he said with open satisfaction. 'And good riddance.'

James couldn't help agreeing, but he couldn't allow Barny to make personal comments about his friends or clients. Of course he knew neither Barny nor Enid liked

Fiona, who had always treated them as servants rather than staff. Her cold arrogance had put their backs up.

Could you blame them? James couldn't but he felt he had to tell Barny off for talking about Fiona that way.

'Don't make personal remarks about my friends,' he said, without real heat.

'No, sir,' Barny said, hurriedly making his face wide-eyed and innocent.

'Hmm,' James murmured, then glanced at his watch and said, 'Hurry up, Barny, I need to get to the hospital quickly.' Patience would have gone there, he was certain of that, and he wanted to arrive before she left; she might not stay long and he would rather not chase her back to her house, where there would be a large audience for anything he tried to say to her. That house was always crowded; you couldn't be alone for two minutes without someone walking in on you and insisting on contributing to the conversation. The word 'privacy' meant nothing to them all.

Although Barny drove as fast as the traffic would permit, it still took them nearly half an hour in rush hour conditions through the busy London streets. Taxis queued at traffic lights, people were mostly going back to their offices from lunch, often flushed and sleepy after too much wine and good food. By the time Barny reached the hospital James was on the edge of his seat.

He raced along the corridors to the ward, flushed and tense, his heart sinking as he opened the door and found his mother alone, propped up against her pillows, listening to the hospital radio on headphones which she immediately took off as he came into the room, a warm smile lighting her pale, drawn face.

'James! They told me you had been while I was

asleep—I was afraid you wouldn't have time to come back today.'

'I made time. I wanted to make sure you were going to be okay. How do you feel now?' He bent to kiss her cheek, breathing in that faint, familiar perfume he remembered from his childhood. Her skin had the soft, wrinkled feel of dried rose petals. She had had bowls of pot pourri around her bedroom with that scent, he thought; whenever he was in there as a very small boy he had been allowed to run his fingers through the contents, letting them trickle back into the bowl slowly, and for ages their scent would cling to his skin. When she'd left his father had had her room cleared and everything in it thrown away. Yet the scents had lingered in the air. Whenever James went into the room even today he thought he could smell them.

She put a hand up to clasp his cheek briefly. 'Much better. They tell me I can go home in a few days. They're keeping me in for observation and rest, but my heart is behaving itself now.'

He pulled up a chair next to the bed and sat down. 'You must take care of yourself after this, though. You don't want to risk another setback, do you?'

She grimaced. 'I certainly don't. I hate hospitals, they're such sad places, especially big ones like this. I'll make sure I don't have to come back here again. Oh, James, thank you for all your lovely flowers—they had to use three vases! I feel as if you've turned this boring ward into a garden for me. I've been lying here since I woke up just gazing and gazing at them. Their scent is marvellous, isn't it?'

He looked at the rather plain, heavy vases arranged around her bed, on her bedside cabinet, on the windowsill nearby. 'The perfume is mostly from the freesias, of course, but I remember you like daffodils.'

' "That come before the swallow dares, and take the winds of March with beauty" ,' she said dreamily.

He frowned, struck by the words, sure he recognised them but not able to place them. 'That's a quotation, isn't it? I'm sure I've heard it before.'

'Shakespeare, James!'

'Is it? It sounds so modern, doesn't it?'

'He often does. I don't think there were any freesias in England in his day, mind you—they're new arrivals in this country, and so are tulips. The Dutch started the craze for tulips, back in the seventeenth century, and it really was a craze—at one time new tulip varieties changed hands for a fortune. Isn't that amazing?'

'You seem to know a lot of odd facts—do you do a lot of crossword puzzles?' There was so much he didn't know about her. They had a lot to learn about each other.

She laughed. 'How did you guess? Patience likes doing crosswords, too.' Gesturing to a bowl of apples, oranges and bananas, she added, 'She brought me all this fruit. I'll never eat it all. A pity to waste it. Have something—one of these tangerines. They're delicious.'

He shook his head. 'No, thanks, I just had lunch.' He paused, then said, trying to sound very casual, 'Patience has been here this afternoon, has she?'

His mother's eyes skimmed his face, sharply narrowed and alert. 'Yes. She didn't stay long; she had to get back. She seemed upset—have you two had words?'

His heart collided with his ribs; breathlessly he said, 'Upset? What made you think she was upset? What did she say?'

His mother put a hand out, covered one of his own;

her skin felt papery and dry but the contact was comforting.

'She didn't say anything; I could tell something was wrong. I'm very fond of Patience. Don't hurt her, James.'

'I wouldn't do that for worlds!' His throat hurt; the words emerged rough and harsh. He drew another audible breath, trying to get himself under control. 'What makes you think I could?'

His mother laughed, distinctly laughed.

'What's so funny?' James couldn't stand being laughed at, especially when he did not get the joke.

'Why don't you ask her yourself, James?'

He was afraid to, but he wasn't admitting that to his mother, so instead he asked her, 'When you come out of hospital, do you want to come home with me, or would you rather stay with Patience?'

She watched him, her wrinkled fingers entwining with his. 'I'm touched that you've asked me that, James, but I could never live in that house again—I was too unhappy there; it would be haunted for me. And I've made so many friends at The Cedars. I'd miss them all if I left. It's the happiest house I've ever lived in; I want to stay there for the rest of my life.'

She wasn't surprising him but he felt he ought to warn her. 'You can't count on that, you know. What if Patience gave up running the house? If she got married, for instance?'

His mother laughed. 'She has promised the children they will never have to leave their home until they are all grown-up, and Emmy is only six. I doubt if I'll still be around by the time she's eighteen.'

James frowned at the floor. 'But what if Patience didn't need to sell The Cedars? What if...say...she married someone with plenty of money? She wouldn't need to take in paying guests then, would she?'

'I can't see her turning Lavinia and Joe and the others out of the house, can you? No matter how much money a possible husband might have.'

His heart sank. 'No, you're right. She's far too soft-hearted.'

'Not soft-hearted, James. Warm-hearted. Generous. Kind. Loving. Patience is a very special person. A man could look for the rest of his life and never find anyone else as special as Patience.'

Their eyes met. He hoped he looked blank as he hurriedly got up. 'Well, I have to get back to the office.' Bending, he kissed her cheek again. 'Is there anything you need? Anything I can get you? I'll see you again tomorrow afternoon.'

'I've got everything I need, thank you, James,' she said with a contented little sigh.

As he walked out of the ward he wished he could say the same. For years he had drifted without any clear idea of what he really needed, let alone having realised that his life was empty, a hollow shell, without loving or being loved.

Too late he had realised the utter necessity of loving, and he was afraid self-knowledge had come too late. He loved Patience, but he had no idea how she felt about him; he didn't understand her at all—why had it taken him so long to see how little he knew about women? Having lost his mother at such an early age had left him blind where women were concerned. He had grown up valuing them for all the wrong reasons, believing a woman should be like Fiona—beautiful, elegant, and cold—whereas the truth was Fiona had been the very opposite of what he needed in a woman. Meeting

Patience had taught him that, but he was still blind and bewildered where women were concerned, especially where Patience was concerned. He was afraid to tell her how he felt in case she turned him down flat. It would hurt too much. He was terrified of getting hurt again.

At the end of the corridor he heard a babble of excitement which resolved itself a moment later into his mother's friends from The Cedars. Lavinia, in a bright blue pleated skirt and matching top, carrying a wicker basket of goodies, Joe in an old tweed jacket and cord trousers, the others talking loudly as they advanced towards him, waving.

'How is she?'

'Patience said she was much better—did you think so too?' asked Lavinia. 'I've made her some of my fatless oatmeal cookies—good for her heart.'

'I brought her some of my daffs,' Joe said, looking discontented. 'I suppose you've already drowned her in expensive flowers from a shop? These are from our own garden.' And she had better prefer them! his belligerent expression said.

'She'll love them,' James hurriedly assured him, looking from Joe to Lavinia. 'And she'll be delighted to see you all. She's missing you already.'

'Are you going to take her home with you when she gets out of here?' asked Joe, still scowling. 'You live in some posh place up West, don't you?'

'I did invite her to move in with me, yes,' admitted James, and saw all their faces fall.

'We'll miss her,' one of the other women said gloomily. 'She fits in with us all. She was going to make me a new nightie.'

'We will miss her,' agreed Lavinia. 'But family is

family, after all. Can't blame her if she wants to live with her own son. We'd all do the same, in her place.'

'But she doesn't want to,' James told them, seeing their faces change, startled and lighting up. 'She thanked me for the thought, but said she would miss your company too much. Enjoy your visit with her. I don't think the ward sister will let you all in at once; my mother has to have a lot of rest at the moment. You'll have to go in two at a time, I expect.'

He waved and walked on and heard them vanishing at their slow pace, talking nineteen to the dozen. His mother would hear them coming long before they arrived. The whole hospital could probably hear them.

'Back to the office?' Barny asked as they drove out of the hospital gate, and James hesitated. That would be the wisest thing to do—go back to work, stay away from Patience—and he had always been discreet and careful in his attitude to life.

Suddenly, though, he felt reckless. There was wildness in the spring air; his grey eyes glittered with it.

'No, I want to go to The Cedars,' he said, and felt Barny flash a curious look at him in his overhead mirror.

'I saw that collection of oldies heading into the hospital. Visiting Madam, of course. I'll be surprised if they let them in. Enough to give a healthy man a heart attack, having that lot descend on him!'

'My mother likes them. She enjoys their company.' James hesitated but decided to be frank with Barny. 'I invited her to come back home to live with me, but she refused. She said she had bad memories of the place, and prefers The Cedars.'

'Ah,' Barny said. 'Well, I can see her point, can't you? I've always thought Number 43 was a gloomy barn of a house, myself. Oh, very elegant and impressive, the decor, but as a home…well, it never was one, was it? When your mother went, we thought of going, too, but we stayed for your sake.'

'God knows what sort of childhood I'd have had without you and Enid. Don't think I'm not grateful.'

'Did we ever ask for gratitude?' growled Barny. 'Enid and me, we always felt we got as much out of it as you did—we had no kids and you made up for that. We were never sorry we did it. You were our family, in a way.'

'And you two were mine,' James quietly said. 'If I got married, Barny, and sold the house, what do you think you and Enid would want to do? Come with me or…?'

'We've been with you so long we're set in our ways, and a new wife feels awkward dealing with staff who've been running things for years. Women like to have their homes arranged the way they like them, and it always leads to bad feelings. No, Enid and me, we've thought about that, and we thought that if you married we'd retire to a nice little flat on the South Coast—maybe Bournemouth—with a sea view and shops nearby.'

'I'd miss you both.'

'We'd miss you, sir, but that's life; nothing stays the same, the world moves on. Sooner or later the work would be beyond us, anyway.'

The car phone began shrilling. Barny glanced round at him. 'Are you here or shall I take it?'

'I'll take it.' James leaned forward to lift the receiver. 'James Ormond here,' he crisply said, and recognised Miss Roper's voice.

'Have you heard the news? Have you got any instructions for me?'

Baffled, James asked, 'What news?'

A silence, then she said carefully, 'About Mr Wallis, sir.'

Fiona's father? His instincts prickled. 'What about him?' Was the old man ill? He was the age to have a stroke or heart attack from overwork, and he had always been obsessed with his business, even since Fiona had joined him. Men like that pushed themselves too far, and one day their bodies gave up the unequal struggle.

'There are rumours going around that he's...' She hesitated, then went on, 'In some sort of financial difficulty.'

James sat up, frowning. 'What does that mean? Don't talk in riddles!'

'Well, it's all very delicate. I don't like to say too much on the car phone; it's so easy for people to eavesdrop. Nobody seems quite sure what is going on. I've had any number of calls from clients who've heard the rumours, and now the press are on to it—I saw an item on the business news on TV just now. They said there was a rumour the Fraud Squad has been called in.'

'The Fraud Squad? That can't be true!'

'It could be. Sir Charles rang to ask what you knew. I told him you were out and asked if he had any definite news. He told me there was some sort of official investigation going on, and he mentioned the Fraud Squad. He said nobody knew where Mr Wallis was. He seems to have vanished. Left the country, Sir Charles said.'

A blinding light hit James. Fiona must have known this news was about to break! No wonder she had seemed desperate. That must be why she had acted out of character, come on so strong to him, tried to seduce him. She had wanted to make him commit himself before he heard about her father.

'Where had Sir Charles got his information? Did he say?'

'Well, not exactly, but Sir Charles did say Miss Wallis was with him; not in the room, but at his house.' Miss Roper's tone was distinctly odd. He picked up a note of suppressed excitement, or satisfaction—or both.

'What on earth was she doing at Charles's place?' he thought aloud. 'Did she go to him for help? Is she involved in whatever her father has been up to?'

'Sir Charles said she was very upset. She had no idea what was going on, and the news of her father's disappearance, and the Scotland Yard investigation of his affairs, had been as big a shock to her as to everyone else.'

'But why was she with Charles, of all people? They've never been close friends—or not that I was aware!'

Miss Roper said softly, 'Well, actually...Sir Charles did tell me they were getting married.'

'What?' James felt as if someone had punched him in the stomach. He gave a loud gasp of incredulity. 'Charles and Fiona?' Charles and Fiona? His mind worked hurriedly, in confusion. Charles had made no secret of fancying Fiona, but his life was crowded with women he desired. He didn't marry any of them. James wouldn't have been amazed to hear Charles had tried to get her into bed, but marriage? That was out of character, just as Fiona's come-on earlier had been out of character.

'Actually, I decided he was ringing you just to give you that news,' Miss Roper told him, dryness in her tone.

Still disbelieving, James demanded, 'Charles actually said they were getting married? I mean, you haven't made any mistake about that? What did he actually say?'

'I am not in the habit of making mistakes when I take messages!' Miss Roper was highly indignant, affronted. 'I assure you, Sir Charles used exactly those words. He said, "We're getting married at once, very quietly." A private wedding in a registry office, just close family, he said. No reception, and then they're going away for a month's honeymoon in the Caribbean on his private yacht.'

'My God,' James said. 'I'm staggered. Charles and Fiona!' He fell silent as he absorbed the news, staring blankly out of the window into the streets of Muswell Hill.

The suburb was set on the northern hills above London's close-set maze. From this height on a clear day you got breathtaking views of the whole city stretching to the horizon: acres of red-tiled and grey-slate-tiled rooftops, chimneys, church spires, concrete tower blocks set in dull grassed landscapes, interwoven with green gardens and trees and city parks, and miles away the bending silvery snake of the Thames sliding off towards the sea with the misty blueish haze of the Kent hills on the far bank of the river. The Victorians had built up here in the belief that the air was clearer and more healthy on these hills, and there was still a rural feel to the place, although since the war there had been a lot more building and the original spaciousness had vanished with infilling and clutter.

'Any instructions?' Miss Roper asked in his ear, and he started.

'What? Oh, yes, you'd better check our involvement with Mr Wallis. He hasn't got any of our money, but go through the files, check which of our clients are also clients of his and get in touch with them to make sure they know there could be problems for them.'

'Are you coming back to the office today?'

'Not for a couple of hours,' he said curtly, still determined to see Patience again before he returned to the office.

'There are a lot of letters to sign, and people have been ringing all day.'

He ignored the discreet reproach in her voice. 'I'll be in touch later this afternoon; hold the fort until then.'

Before she could start to argue he hung up, leaning back in his seat with a frown.

Charles and Fiona! Life was full of these surprises. But, now that he thought about it, he saw that the marriage might well work for both of them. They had similar temperaments and similar interests. Fiona would love having Charles's money to spend and Charles would enjoy having such a young and very beautiful wife.

'Bad news, was it?' Barny asked blandly as he halted at traffic lights, turning his head, his eyes meeting those of his employer.

James regarded him ironically, knowing Barny would have been eavesdropping. 'Bad and good. Miss Wallis is going to marry Sir Charles.'

Unsurprised, Barny nodded; oh, yes, he had overheard every word James said and put two and two together. 'And Mr Wallis, sir? I gathered he was in some sort of trouble.'

'I don't know what Mr Wallis has been up to, but he has apparently vanished from sight.'

They turned into the road where Patience lived and James sat up, his mouth dry, as the car drew up outside The Cedars.

'Shall I wait, sir?'

'Go and have a cup of tea somewhere, or drive around—and come back in an hour, Barny.'

James got out and walked up the drive slowly, trying to decide what to say to Patience when he saw her. The house seemed very quiet—no children or dogs in the garden—but then the children must all be at school, and the old people would all still be at the hospital visiting his mother. What if Patience was out, too? He ground his teeth at the thought; frustration was driving him crazy. He had to talk to her, find out where he stood, how she felt; he couldn't bear to wait any longer.

A second later he heard her voice in the garden, and his heart lifted. She was here! Walking faster, he took the path round the side of the house, urgently looking among the trees for sight of her.

She was closer than he had expected, her red hair gleaming in sunlight, waist slender, breasts small and soft, in old blue jeans and a thin white sweater—and to his fury that boy was with her.

'Colin, try to understand what I'm saying, and don't be so angry!' he heard Patience say, looking up at the boy, who suddenly grabbed her by the waist.

'But I love you!' His voice was shaking, even the hands that held her were trembling visibly. 'I want to marry you—oh, not yet, I know we'll have to wait until I'm earning enough for us to live on, but in a year or two. It won't take as long as my mother says it will.'

Patience sounded distressed. Her voice pleaded, 'Colin, please listen to me!'

She only just got the last word out before the boy was trying to kiss her. Patience struggled, turning her head aside, but the boy kissed every part of her face he could reach—her eyes, her cheeks, her ears, her neck—moaning her name between kisses. 'Oh, Patience, Patience, Patience...'

James wasn't aware of running, or even thinking. Burning with rage, sick with jealousy because that boy was doing what he so badly wanted to do, he yanked the boy off her and held him by the shoulders briefly, shaking him like a rag doll and wanting to hurt him, to hit him hard. The boy struggled, his feet off the ground, until James flung him away to tumble in a heap.

'How can you let him kiss you like that? You know he's too young for you!' James told Patience angrily. 'I may be too old but he's too young!'

She ran towards the boy and helped him up, her arm going round his waist. 'Did he hurt you, Colin?'

'I'll kill him,' the boy shouted, pushing her away and rushing towards James.

'Oh, grow up!' James said through his teeth, and pushed him away again without too much force. Colin stumbled back, clutched at a tree, glaring at him.

'I'm grown up. Don't you think I'm not! And I'm not too young for her! And even if I am...a little...well, I'll get older, but you can never get any younger. Time's on my side; I can wait.'

James flinched at the truth of that, going pale, and couldn't think of a word to say.

Patience was the one who spoke, her voice gently firm. 'Colin, it wouldn't make any difference what age you were! How many more times do I have to tell you? Listen to what I'm saying. Believe me, please believe me—I don't feel that way about you; I never have. I like you—as a friend. I was sorry for you because you were having problems at home—you were unhappy. But that was all it ever was and now I think you should stop coming here. I don't want any more of these scenes. They're getting on my nerves. I don't need all this angst. I have enough of my own problems without having to keep dealing with yours. Go home and find a girl of your own age. Forget all about me.'

The boy stood there, staring at her, his face stricken,

then he turned and tore away without another word. They heard the gate slam behind him.

'Oh, dear,' Patience said unhappily. 'Poor Colin. Why are people so complicated? I kept telling him I didn't love him but he wouldn't listen.'

'As he said, time is on his side. He has a lot of growing up to do. He'll get over you.' James took a deep breath and plunged on huskily. 'I won't. I love you. I've never been in love before, thank God. People tell you how wonderful love is, but they're lying—love hurts. I don't think I can take much more. I might as well have all the pain at once, so if you're going to tell me, too, that you can never feel the same way, say it now and get it over with.'

She looked at him, her eyes wide and luminous, then put a hand to his face, her palm curving over his cheek. 'James…'

'Don't,' he said roughly, pushing her hand down. 'You're talking to me the way you did to that boy I don't want your kindness, Patience, or your sympathy. If you can't love me give it to me straight.'

She considered him, face serious. 'What about your girlfriend? You can't love both of us, James. I saw you kissing her…'

'You saw her kissing me!' he broke out, voice shaking. 'Patience, believe me—Fiona and I were never serious. We dated but we weren't in love, and we never slept together. It was convenient for both of us to have someone to go around with, that was all. We might even have married, some time—but it would have been a terrible mistake. I shudder to think what my life would have been like.'

He could see Patience was not yet convinced. 'Are

you sure she wasn't in love with you? From the way she was kissing you...'

'That was acting! You don't know her. Fiona is cold and clever, very shrewd. She knew by then that I'd changed and she was trying to get me back...'

'And you say she doesn't love you?'

'I know she doesn't. It wasn't me—it was my money Fiona wanted. Her father has run into financial problems and Fiona was desperate to get a rich husband fast.'

'Poor Fiona,' Patience murmured, her face uncertain. 'How can you be so sure she doesn't love you, James? You aren't very good at emotions, are you?'

He had to admit it. 'But I'm certain about Fiona—at lunchtime she was trying to get me to propose, but as we drove here my secretary rang to let me know Fiona had just got engaged to someone else—she made a play for me and failed, so she went on to see a friend of mine, a much older man, with a great deal of money. He rang me to tell me they are getting married at once.'

'You're kidding!' Patience looked staggered.

'Fast work,' agreed James, his mouth curving cynically. 'I told you, her emotions were never involved. Nor were mine. But her marriage might actually work. Charles is very experienced—he's been married several times before—and he isn't in love with her any more than she's in love with him. I knew he fancied her; he made no secret of it. He's very rich, he's much older than her, he won't expect too much and he has no illusions about her. But he'll be generous to her and she'll fit in with his lifestyle and his friends. They might suit each other pretty well.'

Patience looked at him through her lashes. 'You know some very weird people, James. "Cynical and experienced" would describe you, too, wouldn't it?'

He grimaced. 'Cynical, maybe. Experienced? No, I was always too busy. I had no time for love.' He looked at her passionately, his feelings in his eyes. 'Until I met you.'

She ran a finger lingeringly over his mouth, and he drew breath sharply.

'Patience...I love you...'

'Don't talk so much,' she said softly. 'Kiss me.'

James didn't need to be told twice. He framed her face in both his hands and kissed her warm, generous mouth with all the need, desire and emotion inside him.

'I've waited so long to kiss you like this.'

Patience ran her arms round his neck and kissed him back, making his temperature soar. Eyes closed, James held her in his arms, feeling dizzy and yet so happy he could scarcely breathe. Against his chest the soft, high breasts rose and fell in rapid breathing; he thought of burying his face between them, and shuddered with desire.

He felt her lips move under his, whispering his name, then she said in a shaky voice, 'I love you, too, James.'

His heart drove against his breast. 'Do you mean it?' He looked down at her, his eyes feverish with intense feeling.

'Oh, yes. When I left your house today I was so unhappy. Seeing you with that woman made me feel sick. I had to get away. I couldn't bear to pretend, and be polite to her.'

He groaned. 'And I was afraid you had gone because you didn't care!'

'You've no idea how much I cared! I realised I loved you on my birthday. When you arrived, I looked at you and felt quite odd, weak at the knees—it had to be love, although I still wanted to smack you once or twice, when you were being stupid about your mother. I love your mother—she's wonderful; you've got to be nice to her!'

He looked at her with tenderness. 'You're wonderful, do you know that? Will you marry me, Patience? And soon—it has to be soon. Because I'll go out of my mind if I don't get you into bed soon.'

She blushed, making his heart turn over, but then she sighed, her face turning very serious. 'I don't know... I can't, James, I really can't...'

He stiffened, ice trickling down his spine. 'Can't marry me? Why not?' Desperation made his voice roughen, grow harsh. 'If you love me why can't you marry me?'

'If we got married, you'd want me to live in your house, and I can't, James. I can't leave The Cedars, or the children. I promised them we'd always stay here and I can't break my promise. I can't turn my friends out, either; this is their home too, now, and I couldn't dump them back into homes; they'd be so unhappy and I'm very fond of them all.'

He relaxed, sighing with relief. For a moment he had thought she didn't love him enough to marry him.

'I may be stupid about some things, but I've understood the problem of where we would live, Patience, and there's really no problem at all. I've never liked that house in Regent's Park, anyway. I had so little happiness in it. My mother's right—it is haunted, for both of us, her and me. I'll sell the place without a single minute's regret.'

Her face lit up. 'And move in here with us?'

He nodded, smiling at her.

Her eyes were wide and bright for a second, then she said uncertainly, 'Are you sure, James? Could you stand it? You're used to living in a very stately way—your house is so elegant and quiet; you can hear the clocks ticking! This is a madhouse some days, when everyone's home. The children squabbling, the dogs barking, Lavinia and Joe arguing—there's no peace anywhere. It may drive you mad.'

'It probably will, some days, but I can always build myself a treehouse in the garden and go there to get some peace.'

She laughed. 'Emmy wouldn't leave you alone for long. She thinks the sun shines out of you. If you had a private treehouse in the garden she would move in with you.'

'She's adorable,' he said, laughing too. 'When I look at her I know what you looked like at that age.'

'Yes, she is like me! Far more than the boys.' Then Patience sobered again. 'And what about your own staff? Barny and Enid? I liked them so much, James, I wouldn't want to turn them out. They've spent their whole lives looking after you.'

'I talked to Barny just now on the way over here—it seems he and Enid have always wanted to have a flat at Bournemouth with a sea view. They didn't like to leave me in the lurch, but if I get married they'll stop work and find that flat. Apparently they think it's time they retired, anyway.'

Her brow furrowed. 'Did you think he meant it? I mean…are you sure he wasn't just saying what he thought you wanted to hear?'

'I believed him, but you can talk to them yourself, and if you think they don't really want to go we'll work something out. We can always build an extension to The Cedars for them. There's plenty of room here for new building.'

Her eyes gleamed. 'You have an answer for everything, don't you?'

'Patience, if you love me we can work everything else out. All that matters is...do you love me and will you marry me?'

'Yes,' she said huskily. 'Yes, James. I love you, and I will marry you.' She caught his face between her hands and looked up at him with eyes that shone like greeny-blue opals. 'And, James, I can't wait to get you into bed, either.'

Catch more great
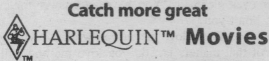
HARLEQUIN™ Movies
featured on the movie channel tmc

Premiering April 11th
Hard to Forget
based on the novel by bestselling
Harlequin Superromance® author
Evelyn A. Crowe

Don't miss next month's movie!
Premiering May 9th
The Awakening
starring Cynthia Geary and David Beecroft
based on the novel by Patricia Coughlin

If you are not currently a subscriber to
The Movie Channel, simply call your
local cable or satellite provider for more
details. Call today, and don't miss out
on the romance!

HARLEQUIN™
Makes any time special.™

100% pure movies.
100% pure fun.

DEBBIE MACOMBER

invites you to the

HEART OF TEXAS

Join Debbie Macomber as she brings you the lives and loves of the folks in the ranching community of Promise, Texas.

If you loved Midnight Sons—don't miss Heart of Texas! A brand-new six-book series from Debbie Macomber.

Available in February 1998 at your favorite retail store.

Heart of Texas by Debbie Macomber

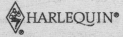

HARLEQUIN®

HARLEQUIN PRESENTS®

Introduces a brand-new miniseries from

Penny Jordan

The Crightons are a family that appears to have
everything—money, position, power and elegance,
but one fateful weekend threatens to destroy it all!

March 1998—THE PERFECT SEDUCTION (#1941)
The Crighton family had been the cause of scandal and
heartache for Bobbie Miller, and she wanted revenge. All she
had to do was seduce Luke Crighton, and the family secrets
would be hers to expose.

April 1998—PERFECT MARRIAGE MATERIAL (#1948)
Tullah was tantalized by her boss, Saul Crighton. A devoted
single father and the sexiest man alive, he was perfect marriage
material. But he plainly didn't see her as the perfect wife!

May 1998—THE PERFECT MATCH? (#1954)
When Chrissie met Guy, she thought her most romantic
fantasies had just come to life. But Chrissie had a family secret
that Guy could surely never forgive....

Available wherever Harlequin books are sold.

HPPJPF